"We're not most people."

"So I'm finding out," Mack sighed.

"Why did you pack up and walk out on me, Mack? All that talk about settling down...the business about a family...That was just a smoke screen—an excuse for leaving me."

"Is that what you think?"

"I—I don't know," Dusty admitted.

"If all I wanted to do was walk out on you, why would I go to all this trouble? I had to track you down and take this flight just to talk to you."

His gaze enveloped her with a wave of intensity that made her limbs weak....

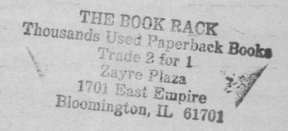

Dear Reader,

Spellbinders! That's what we're striving for. The editors at Silhouette are determined to capture your imagination and win your heart with every single book we published. Each month, six Special Editions are chosen with *you* in mind.

Our authors are our inspiration. Writers such as Nora Roberts, Tracy Sinclair, Kathleen Eagle, Carole Halston and Linda Howard—to name but a few—are masters at creating endearing characters and heartrending love stories. Their characters are everyday people—just like you and me—whose lives have been touched by love, whose dreams and desires suddenly come true!

So find a cozy, quiet place to read, and create your own special moment with a Silhouette Special Edition.

Sincerely,

The Editors
SILHOUETTE BOOKS

PATTI BECKMAN
Danger in His Arms

Silhouette Special Edition

Published by Silhouette Books New York

America's Publisher of Contemporary Romance

With special thanks
to our friends, Marty and Bill

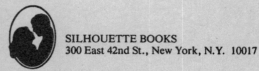

SILHOUETTE BOOKS
300 East 42nd St., New York, N.Y. 10017

Copyright © 1987 by Patti Beckman

ISBN: 0-373-09370-5

First Silhouette Books printing March 1987

America's Publisher of Contemporary Romance

Printed in the U.S.A.

PATTI BECKMAN

has lived the exciting life of many of her heroines. She has been an actress, airline pilot, author and bass player in her husband's jazz band. Her interesting locales and spirited characters will delight her reading audience. She lives with her husband, Charles, and daughter along the coast of Texas.

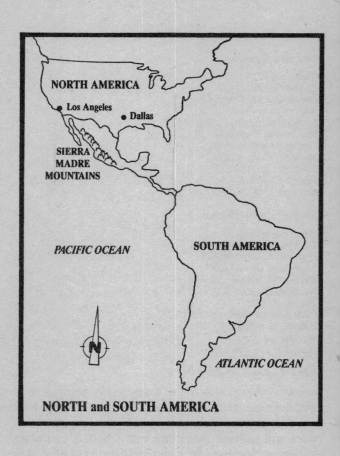

NORTH AMERICA

● Los Angeles ● Dallas

SIERRA
MADRE
MOUNTAINS

PACIFIC OCEAN

SOUTH AMERICA

N

ATLANTIC OCEAN

NORTH and SOUTH AMERICA

Chapter One

A light snow had been falling over the flat Texas countryside since dawn. Dusty Landers gazed morosely through the window of the taxi that was taking her from Dallas to the Dallas-Fort Worth Regional Airport. Gloomily, she thought that the leaden winter sky reflected the somber cloud that had spread over her life these past weeks.

It was hard to believe that her happy, fulfilling life had been altered so drastically. She'd had it all—a successful, exciting career and the man she loved. Now, thanks to that very man, her life had passed through an emotional shredding machine. Tears prompted by mingled hurt and anger stung her eyes.

Thinking about what Mack O'Shea had done to her made her blood boil.

As she furiously dug in her purse for a Kleenex, her hand brushed the bulging camera bag at her side. She gave it an impulsive pat, gaining a measure of comfort from the feel of the smooth, worn leather. The camera was an old buddy; her best friend. It would never let her down. "To hell with you, Mack O'Shea!" she muttered vehemently. "I'll survive. I still have my career. I got along fine before I met you and I'll do it again!"

She directed her attention to the scenery outside in an effort to distract herself. It was depressing to dwell on Mack and the muddle that was her life.

The Texas prairie, lightly dusted with snow, stretched as far as the eye could see. In the distance was the skyline of Fort Worth. On the opposite horizon was Dallas. Less than twenty-four hours before, she had taken off from JFK airport in New York. After having arrived in Dallas, she had spent several intense hours interviewing and photographing one of the most famous rock-music stars in the world. Now she was on her way to California to do a story on the macho movie star, producer and writer, Grant Packer. Half the female population would cut their wrists to be in her place. And after that interview, on to China, perhaps, or the mideast...wherever a hot event or breaking story led her. Free-lance photojournalists like herself had no time to sit around and mope, or to think about what might have been.

Dusty's pulse quickened as the taxi pulled up to the curb. It was a feeling she often experienced when arriving at one of the world's great airports. She paid the taxi driver, slung the strap of her camera bag over her shoulder, tucked her purse under one arm and with her free hand grasped the handle of her suitcase. Accustomed to jetting all over the world as she was, she had learned how to travel light.

In the main lobby of the giant terminal, Dusty was engulfed within a tide of humanity. She saw women in saris, men in European-style business suits and Italian shoes, an Arabian in a suit but with his traditional sheikh headgear, Texas oil millionaires in cowboy boots and broad-brimmed hats, women in blue jeans and in furs fresh off the racks of Neiman-Marcus. French, Arabian and Spanish interspersed with Texas drawls echoed from all directions.

In the sea of faces, Dusty recognized the marks of human drama—love, loneliness, fatigue, excitement.

More than one man turned for a second look as Dusty passed by. They saw a young woman of extraordinary good looks, slightly taller than average, dressed in boots, jeans, plaid shirt and trench coat carrying an elaborate camera bag slung over a shoulder. They saw a lithe figure, long legs and wide shoulders. But it was the face that attracted the second look. From a full-blooded Cherokee Indian grandmother she had inherited a cloud of black hair, jet-black eyes, high cheekbones, full lips and a complexion with just a hint of bronze.

Dusty joined the long line threading its way to the ticket counter. Overhead, large monitors displayed flight information. She ran her gaze down the list and saw that her California flight was scheduled to leave on time.

Eventually she reached the counter, where she checked her suitcase and got her ticket and boarding pass. Turning, she started toward the gate.

Suddenly a broad-shouldered giant of a man crowded his way into her line of vision. Dusty froze in her tracks. The sounds around her dissolved into a throbbing hum. Her pulse sounded like a tom-tom in her ears. Her mouth went dry.

"Hello, Dusty," the man murmured in a slow, drawling baritone. Although he spoke softly, his words drowned out the myriad other sounds in the vast terminal lobby.

For a moment, Dusty was paralyzed, her vocal chords frozen. Then, somewhere in her confusion, she found her voice. "Mack O'Shea, what in hell are you doing here?"

That was her first startled reaction, quickly followed by a torrent of violent emotions that had her shaking from head to foot.

A slow, infuriating grin spread over the big man's rugged countenance. "Why, I'm doing what most people in an airport do—I'm catching a plane."

Dusty's eyes filled with bitter tears. How dare he behave so casually? Was she just now discovering a streak of uncaring cruelty among the other disillusioning facets of his character? How could she ever have thought she knew this man she had once loved with such total commitment? How could she have surrendered to him with such abandon? How could she have believed she would love him forever? Why, she hadn't known him at all. She was looking at a stranger. The wedding ring on her finger became a hot branding iron that burned her flesh. What a sentimental fool she had been to continue wearing it after he'd left her. But maybe she'd be glad she did. Now she had an opportunity to snatch it off and hurl it in his face.

Suddenly his big hand closed around her arm and he began steering her toward one of the coffee shops in the main lobby.

"What are you doing?" she demanded.

"I'm going to treat you to a cup of coffee," he said, speaking in the slow, soft drawl that used to turn her insides to butter.

But she wasn't going to fall for that old magic this time. Not after the dirty trick he'd pulled on her. She jerked her arm free. "No, you are not. I have a plane to catch."

"You have plenty of time."

"No, I don't!"

"Sure you do. Your flight doesn't leave for another twenty minutes."

"How would you know that? You don't even know what flight I'm on."

"You're on the ten-thirty plane to Los Angeles. I have a seat on the same flight."

Her mouth fell open. "You have a seat on the same..."

It occurred to her that this was too much of a coincidence. In fact it wasn't a coincidence at all! He'd come to the airport looking for her. But how could he know she would be here this morning? How could he know what flight she was taking?

"What are you up to, Mack O'Shea?"

"Let's have that coffee," was all he would say.

Seated at a Formica-topped table, Dusty wrapped her chilled fingers around the warm cup. Mack was seated across from her in the small booth. She was acutely aware of his gaze engulfing her. His presence was overpowering.

She stole a glance at this big, slow-talking man who could turn into a walking demolition squad if aroused, and yet could be so clumsily tender that it wrenched her heart. Would she ever rid herself of her obsession for him? How was it possible that she could still feel a wave of the old sweet tenderness, the longing, the desire? A flood of bittersweet memories threatened to overwhelm her.

It had been a month since they'd last made love. The fog had been dense that night in London. She remembered it too clearly—the quiet corner pub, the secluded booth, the drinks, the sudden look that passed between them, the touch of his hand, the delicious shudder that ran through her body. Then the two of them, hand in hand, running laughing and carefree as children through the fog to the small hotel. In their room, their clothes scattered on the floor, Mack's strong arms around her, his mouth hungry on hers, her frantic answering kiss, the burning touch of his bare flesh against hers, the total abandonment, the ecstasy, the climactic fulfillment and then the soft, tender cuddling in his powerful arms, the peace and security, his slow, rumbling baritone groping awkwardly for the words to express his deepest feelings.

Now the memory of that last night with him warmed her body, swelling her breasts, making her long to press her leg against his hard muscular thigh under the table, to slide her palm into his lap in the old intimacy.

Then the memory of the morning after returned, the memory of the argument in the cold light of dawn...the argument that had been brewing for a month. Her heart had been torn right out of her when she'd come back from the Cairo assignment two weeks later to find he had moved out of their New York apartment, leaving nothing behind except a brief, cold note. The desolation of that morning washed over her. She thought about how she had wandered through the apartment like a lost child, staring at the empty racks in the closet where his clothes had hung, longing desperately for the familiar, comforting sight of them. But they were gone, as were his books, his country-and-western record collection, his shaving gear, all the personal things that were a part of Mack O'Shea. It had been as if he had never existed, as if their apartment had never been their home for the past two years.

The icy chill returned, making her furious with herself for feeling any remainder of tender love and fiery passion.

"I suppose you've started your job with the Nicholson Corporation," she said coldly.

He nodded thoughtfully. "Yes, I have."

"That should make Laura very happy. When are the two of you getting married?"

He gave her a penetrating look. "I'm still married to you, remember?"

"Not for long. Before I left New York I told my lawyer to start divorce proceedings."

Surprise flared in his angry eyes. "You sure didn't waste any time."

"Not any more than you did when you moved out."

Black eyes clashed with blue during a moment of steaming silence. Mack took a sip of his coffee, a dark scowl on his rugged features. She thought that if looks could kill, they'd both be sprawled out on the coffee-shop floor, dead.

"I never want to see you again, Mack O'Shea," she said, fighting back her tears. "I almost didn't take this Dallas assignment for fear I might run into you. But Dallas is a big city, I told myself, and I'll give the Nicholson Corporation a wide berth. Now I want to know how you found out I'd be catching this Los Angeles flight."

He looked surprised, then shrugged. "Easy. I called Myra, your agent."

Of course. How could she expect to hide from an ex-CIA agent?

"Why did you bother?"

"I'm beginning to wonder myself," he growled. Then he shrugged. "I wanted to talk to you. But there's no use talking to a Cherokee on the warpath."

"No more than trying to talk to an Irishman when he gets stubborn," she fired back.

There was another heavy silence. Finally, relenting, she asked, "What did you want to talk to me about?"

"I wanted to see if you'd come to your senses. But if you've filed for divorce, I guess I have my answer."

"Come to my senses!" she cried. "You're the one who messed everything up. We were getting along fine until you started all the trouble. Or maybe," she said bitterly, "Laura started all the trouble."

He shook his head. "Leave Laura out of this."

"Why should I? We both know you made a mistake marrying me when you were still in love with her. That's what's really behind our breakup, isn't it? Why aren't you man enough to admit it, Mack O'Shea?" She was fighting a desperate battle to hide her tears.

Mack looked furious, but their bitter argument was interrupted by the announcement of their flight.

"You're going to fool around and make me miss my plane," she said angrily, grabbing up her purse and camera bag.

"Yeah, it would be the end of the world if you didn't get to Hollywood in time to interview Grant Packer."

"Myra has a big mouth. Is there anything about my schedule she didn't tell you? I'm going to have to talk to her about giving my itinerary to strangers."

"Strangers? Dusty, I'm your husband."

"Not much longer."

Dusty slung her camera bag over her shoulder and stalked out of the coffee shop without a backward look, not wanting him to see the streaming tears she could no longer control.

She made her way blindly to a rest room, where she repaired her tear-streaked face and regained control of her emotions. Then she went on to the security gate where she had her usual argument with the security people, who wanted to run her camera bag under the X-ray scanner. "I've got thirty rolls of film in there," she snapped.

"It won't hurt your film, lady."

"Don't give me that guff, buster. I've been through every airport security check in the world. I've had this same argument in seven different languages. Those X rays might wipe out my film. You hand check that camera equipment or let me talk to your superior."

The guard shrugged good-naturedly and opened the bag. She waited impatiently while he unscrewed the lens caps of her Nikons and looked through the viewfinder. He opened every box of film and checked the contents. Meanwhile she set her purse on the conveyor belt and then walked through the metal-detector archway.

On the other side, she was handed her camera bag and purse. Then she started down the long corridor lined with snack bars and gift shops to the waiting area.

She walked right into the jetway and onto the plane, immediately locating her window seat. Since the magazine that had given her the Grant Packer assignment was paying her travel expenses, she could afford first class.

She had hardly gotten settled before a male passenger took the seat beside her. She looked at him and gasped.

"How did you arrange that?" she demanded. But before Mack could reply, she answered for him. "I know—with the weight Nicholson Corporation has, they can arrange anything. Didn't I read somewhere that Robert Nicholson is now in the billionaire class— one of the five richest men in the country?"

"Don't get sarcastic, Dusty," Mack remonstrated as if to an outspoken child. "Bob Nicholson is a good friend who has given me a fine job."

"I'm sure his daughter, Laura, had something to do with that," she said cuttingly.

"You just won't leave that alone, will you?"

"Why should I? After all, you were engaged to her when you met me."

"That has nothing to do with Bob giving me this job. It has nothing to do with us."

"Oh, doesn't it? Why else did you pack up and walk out on me, Mack O'Shea?"

"Maybe if you'd get off the warpath long enough for us to have a sensible conversation, I'd explain why."

"Don't talk to me about being sensible. You stopped being sensible several months ago."

He scowled. "Why? Because I want something of a normal life, a place I can come home to every night after work? A family? Isn't that what most people consider sensible?"

"We're not most people."

"So I'm finding out."

Dusty turned away to gaze out the window and watch the passing scenery as the big engines thundered to life. The plane began a long, lumbering taxi along a runway that took them over a freeway before it began to pick up speed and then smoothly took off. Below, Fort Worth and Dallas became miniature cities. The plane reached flight altitude and the voice of their pilot was heard briefly over the speaker system welcoming them aboard the flight, relating flight details and the time they would be landing in L.A.

A woman flight attendant moved down the aisle, taking orders for drinks. Some passengers began reading magazines, others chatted with their companions or dozed.

Dusty sighed as she diverted her attention from the window. Feeling lonely and betrayed, she looked down at her fingers spread on her lap. "All that talk about settling down...the business about a family...that was just a smoke screen—an excuse for leaving me."

"Is that what you think?"

Her dark eyes, filled with hurt and anger, blazed at him. "What else am I supposed to think?"

"If all I wanted to do was walk out on you, why would I go to all this trouble to track you down?"

"I—I don't know," she admitted.

His intense gaze enveloped her and made her limbs weak. She tried to drag her eyes away, but failed. Then he leaned closer and captured her hand in his big, strong fingers. His voice was low, keeping the words private from nearby passengers. "Dusty, you stubborn little idiot, the reason I packed up and moved out was to try and jolt some sense into you. You were in Cairo when Bob Nicholson called to confirm the job. I had to get my tail to Dallas right away. I knew if I called you about it, we'd just have the same old dead-end argument again. I was hoping actions might work where words have been failing."

Dusty stared at him and tried to sort out her feelings. "You thought I'd come running after you?" she asked incredulously.

"Not with your stubborn pride," he said, shaking his head. "But I hoped at least you'd make some effort to contact me. You'd have seen I'm committed to this move and maybe you would have been willing to compromise." Then his words took on a bitter edge. "Instead, you went running to a divorce lawyer."

She lowered her eyes. For two weeks she'd been wrapped up in her own self-pity and wronged indignation. Now he was suddenly making her feel guilty.

She thought about the reason for their estrangement. How was it possible that two such utterly different individuals could fall in love and get married? Mack was slow-talking, deliberate, thoughtful. Her moods were mercurial. She talked a lot. He was sparing with his words. She moved fast. He was like a lumbering bear. She acted on impulse. He planned his moves carefully.

Pain constricted her throat; tears blurred her eyes. "Maybe it would be for the best, Mack," she said sadly. "Somehow our lives have gone off in different directions. You knew when you married me how important my career is to me. The excitement, the challenge...I thrive on it. And there's the wonderful feeling of accomplishment and fulfillment when I see my byline, knowing people all over the world are reading my work. And you're asking me to give all that up to lead a routine life as a homemaker. I'm too young, Mack. I want to taste the glory for a few more years...then there'll be plenty of time for raising a family—"

"Nobody's asking you to turn into a routine housewife," Mack pointed out. "You're a first-class photographer. You could open a studio or publish a book of your photographs or start a business. A lot of women combine motherhood with professional careers. I just want us both to stop chasing all over the world, grabbing a weekend together when our schedules happen to meet. I'm tired of wondering every time I see you off on a plane if I'm going to see you alive again...."

"You knew what it was going to be like when we got married," Dusty pointed out. "We both accepted the risks...."

"Maybe I started revising my priorities."

What confused her so much was that she knew Mack would make a wonderful father. She could just see him beaming with love and pride as he held a cute little daughter on his lap or played sandlot baseball with a son. A fresh wave of guilt engulfed her. How could she deny him that fulfillment? She wasn't being fair.

But was it fair to sacrifice her career at this time in her life? At thirty-two, Mack had had his share of thrills and excitement. He'd tasted the danger and experienced the glory. Now he was ready to settle down. But at twenty-four, she yearned for adventure. In a few years, she'd have it out of her system. Then she'd want a family, too. But not yet. What would it do to her if she turned her back on her own feelings? In all likelihood, she'd begin to resent Mack and the change he'd forced on her. She'd miss the thrills, the excitement, the satisfaction of her career.

His big, strong fingers tightened around her hand, sending an electric current up her arm. Then he leaned even closer. His gaze trailed from her eyes to her lips, down to the top button of her blouse and back to her eyes.

She was finding it increasingly hard to breathe. Her senses were heightened, aware of his body warmth, the rugged planes of his face, the weather-beaten texture of his skin, the masculine scent of his body mingled with a leather-and-spice shaving lotion.

In a low voice barely audible to her, he murmured, "Remember that last night we had together in London? You can't fool me, Dusty. You want me as much as ever right now. You're hooked on me just like I'm hooked on you."

A thousand tender memories flooded her mind. Being married to Mack O'Shea had been a stormy experience. When they hadn't been fighting, they'd been on a continuous honeymoon. He'd be off somewhere in the mideast or Central America on a CIA assignment. She'd be on the other side of the globe covering a story. Then they would find a few days they could steal for themselves. They would meet in Berlin or Rome or Tokyo. Once, a friend of Mack's on the south coast of France had loaned them his sailboat and they had spent a glorious week of sun-drenched days and romantic nights.

She found herself desperately wanting his arms around her, his lips on hers.

He's right, damn it. I am hooked on him. But it didn't solve a blasted thing. It only made the situation more impossible. How nice it would be just to get a divorce and forget that Mack O'Shea had ever existed. How it would simplify things....

Suddenly her train of thought was distracted by a disturbance in the aisle. Mack pulled away and turned while Dusty looked over the back of her seat. She saw a woman flight attendant struggling with a man. Then a second man came running up the aisle. Events began happening fast.

The first man swung his hand, viciously hitting the flight attendant, throwing her to her knees. Then he looked around with a wild-eyed, half-insane expression. His hand held a gun. The second man had run to the front of the aisle. He was shouting as he, too, waved a gun.

Dusty had seen that look too often not to know what it meant; she had seen it on the faces of Iranian fanatics; she had seen it in faces of Shiite Moslems; she had seen it on the face of a man at a terrorist murder trial.

"My God," she choked. "We're being hijacked!"

Chapter Two

Dusty had been in life-threatening situations more than once in her career. Always there seemed a kind of unreality about them.

How could this be happening? How could they be traveling peacefully one minute and be in a shattering crisis the next?

A part of her experienced the danger and reacted with fright. At the same time, another part of her—that part conditioned by professional experience—was somehow detached as if she were viewing the drama through a camera lens, seeing the pale, stricken faces of the passengers, the look of terror on the face of the woman flight attendant who was forced at gunpoint by one of the hijackers to the pilot's flight deck.

Like the cool professional she was, she wondered how, with such tight security at the airport, something like this could happen.

There were two men, each armed with heavy-calibre handguns, probably .357 Magnums, she gauged. The man roughly pushing the flight attendant ahead of him had forced her to use her key to unlock the pilot's compartment. The other man was moving up and down the aisles. He was waving his gun and shouting commands and threats in broken English, ordering the passengers to remain in their seats and not make a sudden move. Dusty heard muffled sobs from some of the frightened passengers.

"How in blazes did they get those guns through security?" Dusty asked Mack under her breath.

He shrugged. "Maybe they had some inside help," he muttered. "A baggage handler might have smuggled the guns on board while the plane was being serviced."

She saw him staring at the hijackers intently. Like a true ex-CIA agent, he was memorizing a photographic image of them while he measured their moves and weighed chances of overpowering them.

"Don't do something crazy," she whispered. But then she knew Mack wouldn't; he didn't operate on impulse as she did. His moves were carefully thought out. He wouldn't attempt any kind of move against the hijackers unless the chances of success were on his side. Then, heaven help the hijackers. It was for good reason that, during his pro-football career, Mack O'Shea had been called "the Slammer."

She quietly rearranged her folded trench coat, holding it on her lap, her hand edging toward the pocket that contained a range-finder camera. It was completely automatic: automatic focus, automatic advance. All she had to do was catch the picture in the viewfinder, snap the shutter and duck the camera back under her trench coat. She could do it in two seconds.

Could she pull it off without the hijacker noticing?

Mack took his eyes off the hijackers for a moment to glance at her. Was he reading her mind? She was so close to him that perhaps he'd felt her body tense. She knew he'd slug her if he guessed what she was planning to do.

The captain's voice came over the loudspeaker, interrupting her thoughts. He was making an effort to keep a professional calm tone but she heard the undercurrent of tension. "I am sorry to inform you that a situation has arisen that has caused us to change our flight plans. We have changed course due south and are presently flying over Mexico. Our destination is Central America...."

Dusty heard gasps of dismay from the frightened passengers.

"...Please remain seated and keep calm. No one will be injured...."

I wish I could believe that, Dusty thought grimly, remembering with a cold chill the look in the hijacker's eyes. It was the look of a trapped animal—deadly, wary, tense to the point of hysteria. She watched him now as he roamed with the deadly weapon clutched in his hands. His face glistened with perspiration. His shirt was soaked with it. He was like an explosive charge that could be set off by the slightest provocation.

She wondered what was going on in the flight deck, where the other hijacker had taken control of the crew. Was he letting them use the radio? Was the plane being tracked on radar?

So far, no demands had been made, only that the plane change direction to Central America.

Dusty glanced around at the passengers in her section of the plane, detailing the dramatic scene in case she lived to write the story. No, she corrected herself, *when* she wrote the story. Falling victim to hopeless fear in a crisis like this was a fatal trap.

She coped with her fear by writing the story in her mind. She described the elderly couple across the aisle—the dignified white-haired gentleman tenderly comforting his wife, who was sobbing softly; the little girl behind them, her face pale, clutching her doll, her mother's arm around her, shielding her with her body. Behind them was a tired-faced, defeated-looking middle-aged man in a rumpled business suit. He had been drinking steadily since the plane had taken off. He'd been holding a fresh drink when the hijackers had taken over the plane. Now he raised it to his lips with a trembling hand. Next to him was a husky young man in a bright orange sweater, scowling at the hijacker, showing no fear, only anger.

Looking down the aisle, seat by seat, Dusty cataloged the victims, reading emotions in their eyes, imagining their personal lives. There was a young couple holding hands tightly. Were they on their honeymoon? An older man, deathly pale, thrust a tablet under his tongue. Nitroglycerine? A handsome man was wearing an expensive suit and had a country-club tan, a streak of distinguished gray at the temples and a tooled leather briefcase on his lap. Hollywood producer? Advertising executive? Then a nun, her eyes closed as she fingered her beads. Two frightened young women looked like secretaries on vacation. An older man, casually dressed, tanned, white-haired and in his sixties, but still trim and vigorous, had a wry smile on his lips as if he were encountering an old acquaintance—death—again. Dusty imagined him as a World War II veteran, perhaps a fighter pilot remembering dogfights over the English Channel when life could be over in a matter of seconds.

She looked at the people and she watched the hijacker. At the same time her hand closed over the hard outlines of the camera that she had now slipped out of her trench coat pocket. What a fantastic picture this would make. The medley of expressions—fright, anger, resignation—frozen at the snap of the shutter. She could catch the hijacker—swarthy, bearded, as menacing as some dark force of evil. A picture of a major hijacking in progress. What a scoop! Every newspaper, every publishing company in the country would fight for it. A photograph like that might win her a Pulitzer prize.

Personal interests aside, such a photograph could be of value to the FBI in identifying the hijackers in the event that they pulled this off and escaped.

It was an opportunity she could not ignore. Every fiber of her professional being challenged her to take the dare.

She had the camera ready. She knew she could do it with one hand. A single upward sweep with her right hand, a twist and rapid rise in her seat, a squeeze of the shutter. Then she would duck the camera back under her coat. The muffled sounds of the sobbing passengers and the whine of the plane's engines would probably be enough to cover the soft click of the shutter.

The camera had a fairly wide-angle lens that would capture most of the scene she wanted. It was loaded with fast film so the rapid shutter speed could freeze motion in a split second; she needn't be too concerned about holding the camera steady.

Every muscle in her body tensed. She took a deep breath and held it. Now her complete attention was zeroed in on the hijacker. She had to choose her moment precisely, when he was slightly turned away so he wouldn't see the camera, yet so she could catch his face in stark profile. He was constantly on the move, prowling the aisle like a restless predator, snarling at the passengers to be quiet, watching with an eagle eye for anything he would consider a threatening move.

Now!

She made her move in one swift, smooth motion. The camera to her eye. The click of the shutter. Camera back under her coat.

But not quick enough.

Either he heard the shutter or caught sight of her hurried movement.

With the guttural snarl of an enraged beast, the hijacker spun around, his gun raised. She saw the black hole of the muzzle, a deadly eye staring straight at her. She saw the man's glare wild with fury, his teeth bared. Her throat tightened as the man's finger whitened on the trigger.

She was going to die.

She went numb with terror, frozen in her seat.

Suddenly Mack O'Shea lunged from the seat beside her, moving so fast that she only saw a blur, heard a muffled shout. Somebody screamed. Was it her?

She was on her feet, coat and camera spilling to the floor, her icy fingers pressed to her face, eyes wide, as she saw Mack grappling with the hijacker. In one blinding instant, he'd grabbed the hijacker's wrist, pushing the gun toward the ceiling.

Then the tired-looking man in the rumpled business suit gulped the remainder of his drink, got up and kicked the hijacker's leg behind his knee, throwing him off balance. At the same time, the husky-looking young man in the orange sweater came out of his seat with a grunt and encircled the hijacker's throat with one powerful arm. Mack wrenched the gun free and delivered a punch to the man's midsection that knocked all the wind out of him. They pushed him to the floor and the orange-sweatered young man sat on him.

Dusty crumpled into her seat, trembling violently. She gulped ragged breaths, trying to regain control.

Mack had the pistol now. He had taken complete command of the situation. He snapped quick orders to the passengers around them. Dusty couldn't quite comprehend how a guy as big and lumbering and clumsy and slow-talking as Mack O'Shea could move so fast and give orders so rapidly.

Several men supplied belts to tie the hijacker's arms and legs. Someone stuffed a handkerchief in his mouth to keep him quiet.

The young man in the orange sweater got up off the man. "Thanks," Mack said to him.

"You're Mack O'Shea, aren't you?" the husky fellow said. He held out a hand. "Jack Sampson. Texas U. all-American fullback. I watched you play tackle with the Dallas Cowboys when I was in grade school. You were one of my idols."

"Nice to meet you, Jack. Appreciated the assistance."

Then Mack turned to Dusty. The look in his eyes made her shrivel inside.

"I ought to put you across my knee and whip the daylights out of you!" he said furiously. "That damn camera of yours nearly got us all killed!"

The camera! Frantically, she scrambled for it. Then she had it in her hands, shooting pictures as fast as the automatic film advance would operate. She saw it all vividly through the viewfinder, the hijacker on the floor, bound hand and foot, the young football player in the orange sweater, the man in the rumpled suit who had produced a small flask out of a coat pocket, the looks of shock and relief on the passengers' faces. Every time the shutter clicked she felt a surge of pleasure.

Mack's big hand closed around her wrist, pulling the camera down. She stared into his furious eyes.

"Don't you ever think about anything but that damned camera?"

"I'm not causing any problem taking pictures now," she retorted.

He pushed her roughly into her seat. His finger pointed at her seemed as menacing as the hijacker's gun. "You stay put," he warned. "I can't cope with this situation and you at the same time."

Her eyes narrowed angrily. "You can't order me around, Mack O'Shea!"

Their gazes locked in momentary combat, his blue eyes flashing lightning, the depths of hers black with defiance.

"How would you like to get yourself tied up like the hijacker?"

"You wouldn't dare!" she gasped.

"Yeah? Try me."

Something in his expression told her he might do just that. She momentarily backed down.

Mack turned to the passengers who had crowded around him. He was obviously some kind of professional who knew what to do in this situation, and they looked to him for leadership.

"I want everybody to stay seated and be as calm as possible. I'm going to break into the flight deck and try to surprise the other hijacker."

Dusty's heart stopped beating. Forgotten was her anger of a moment before. The enormity of the risk sent a cold shudder through her body. Her voice was unsteady. "Mack, no... you'll get your fool head blown off!"

"I don't think so," he said calmly. "I have the element of surprise on my side. The man in there has no idea what has happened out here. He's probably very busy standing guard over the crew and giving them orders. He'll undoubtedly be facing them, with his back to the door. Those cockpit doors are very flimsy, I can snap the lock with a kick and grab the guy before he knows what hit him."

Several men pushed forward to offer their help, but Mack smiled wryly. "This has to be a one-man end-line run."

He turned the hijacker's gun over to the all-American fullback. "Do you know how to use one of these?"

Jack Sampson nodded. "I've won several trophies in target shooting."

"Well, this is no clay pigeon, so be careful. I want you to crouch beside the door. Don't get trigger-happy unless the guy in there gets the best of me and the crew and comes out shooting. Then you'd better hit the bull's-eye the first shot."

Dusty was aware of a sick feeling in the pit of her stomach. She looked at Mack through a blur of tears; how she loved him and how desperately afraid she was. If there was any way she could possibly stop him, she would, but the set of his jaw and the determined look in his eyes convinced her he'd never listen.

Instead, she rose and put her hand on his arm. "Mack..." Her voice was unsteady.

He turned to her. Their eyes met.

She swallowed hard, but she couldn't put her thoughts into spoken words.

Their eyes held for one agonizing, parting moment and then he went for the door. He gave it a savage kick, breaking the latch. Without a second's hesitation, he plunged into the cabin.

Afterward, Dusty was never able to sort out the events of the next sixty seconds—the shouting curses, the ear-shattering blast of gunfire, the strange shock that ran through the entire plane, then a sideways lurch of the huge craft that spilled passengers from their seats and caused luggage to tumble into the aisles. Then there was an unearthly rushing sound from the flight cabin and papers, dust and small objects began swirling around in the air.

Clutching her camera, Dusty stumbled to the demolished cabin door right on the heels of Jack Sampson. She was terrified that she would see Mack lying on the floor in a pool of blood. Wide-eyed, she took in the unbelievable sight of the cabin in a glance.

Far from dead, Mack was on the floor, wrestling with the hijacker. The awful rushing sound came from the shattered front window on the captain's side. He looked stunned, slouched over, his face covered with blood. In the copilot's seat, the first officer was struggling with the controls, trying to get the jet back on a level course.

Jack Sampson helped Mack subdue the hijacker while the second officer, the flight engineer, sprang from his seat and went to the captain's aid.

Dusty heard the first officer shouting, "We're depressurizing. Get everyone on oxygen until I get this thing down to five thousand feet."

The woman flight attendant who had been forced into the cabin with the hijacker was in a state of shock, sobbing hysterically, but the senior flight attendant had come running into the cockpit and was now grabbing the intercom microphone and relaying the message to the passengers. Then she and the flight engineer helped the half-stunned captain out of his seat. Dusty saw that his face had been cut up by flying debris. "Let's get him back to the passenger section for first aid," the senior flight attendant snapped. She looked like a seasoned veteran who was steady as a rock in any kind of emergency.

Dusty crouched back against a wall while she snapped some fast pictures. Her breathing was becoming labored and her head was swimming. Then she felt herself being shoved roughly into a seat and an oxygen mask was clamped over her face. She sucked oxygen into her starved lungs. Her vision cleared and she saw Mack standing over her. He looked disheveled. His shirt was torn and there was an ugly bruise on his chin.

Dusty pushed the oxygen mask aside for a moment. She tried to ask him if he was all right, but it was impossible to make herself heard over the dreadful rushing of the wind blasting through the shattered window that seemed to make the whole jet stagger and lurch.

Over the terrible noise, she heard the copilot shouting, "That broken window is creating a powerful drag on the plane. We've got a dangerous situation here. I have to land right away."

Mack grabbed Dusty's arm and half-dragged her back to a seat in the passenger section. There he fastened her seat belt. The aftermath of the violence had left her temporarily drained. She didn't feel like putting up an argument.

The two hijackers were tied securely and placed in seats with safety belts fastened.

Mack went back to the flight deck. While he was gone, the flight attendant's voice came over the loudspeaker, announcing that they were now below five thousand feet so it was no longer necessary to use the emergency oxygen masks.

Shortly after that Mack returned, taking his seat beside Dusty. He looked pale and strained. "The copilot says he has to land. He hasn't any choice. That open window has created too much of a drag to maintain flight speed for any distance."

Dusty's mouth went dry. She was afraid of what the answer was going to be, but she asked anyway. "Are we near an airport with a runway long enough to handle a big jet?"

Mack shook his head. "We're not near any kind of airport. We're somewhere over a remote section of the Sierra Madre mountain chain in Mexico. He has to make a forced landing."

Dusty swallowed hard. "In the mountains?"

"When we get below these clouds, he's hoping to find some kind of plateau."

She felt a sick knot in the pit of her stomach.

The flight attendant's voice came over the speakers. "Please listen carefully. Because of the damage to the aircraft, it is necessary that we make an emergency crash landing. The first officer has spotted some level terrain. We're circling now and in a few minutes will land. Therefore we are asking everyone to make certain your seat belts are fastened and then to assume a crash position with your heads down on your laps. The landing is going to be rough but we'll make it. As soon as the aircraft stops, the doors will be opened and we'll evacuate the aircraft with the emergency slides. Please try to be calm and orderly when we evacuate the plane. Don't panic...don't rush and we'll be able to get you safely to the ground."

Dusty's body went rigid at the thought...crash landing!

Chapter Three

Like a great, wounded bird, the huge jet swept down toward a rocky plateau high in the Mexican Sierras. The naked belly of the plane swooped over the rough earth and then touched it with a tortured scream. Sparks flew and metal ripped.

"Bend over and grab your ankles!" the flight attendants shouted.

Dusty felt her body jerked violently against her seat belt. Screams mingled with the clatter and metallic crashing of the enormous plane jolting over the ground. Completely out of control now, the jet wallowed grotesquely; metal was ripped from the wings and underbelly.

There was a final, earsplitting crash as the nose of the plane smashed into a giant outcropping of stone, bringing the craft to a jarring stop.

For a ghastly moment there was a stunned silence as if the plane and everyone aboard were dead in the sudden darkness. But then the cabins became filled with cries of fright and pain.

Half-dazed, Dusty fumbled with her seat belt. She heard Mack's voice. "Are you all right?" he repeated.

She nodded, drawing a ragged breath. "I think so. How about you?"

"Okay. Now let's get out of here."

The flight attendants had scrambled out of their seats as soon as the plane had come to a halt, and had hurried to the doors. The jet was leaning to one side. Dusty struggled out of her seat and moved along a tilted aisle, holding the back of seats for support. She and Mack were the first to reach a cabin door behind a flight attendant.

The uniformed young woman was struggling with the heavy door. She rotated the door handle to her right. Jet-aircraft doors were made to open inward first then swing out, which worked fine on a level runway. But with the plane tilted as it was, the heavy door came swinging in, knocking her against Mack and Dusty.

She was a slight young woman and there was no way she could budge the heavy door. Mack threw his two-hundred-pound brawn into the struggle. They rocked the door back and forth and it went swinging out. Only at that point, when icy drops pelted her face from the open doorway, did Dusty realize that they had landed in a freezing rain.

The evacuation slide had been released automatically from the encasement. The flight attendant yanked a red loop, inflating the slide. There was a hissing sound as the yellow canvas slide unfolded and snapped into position, taut and straight.

The interior of the plane was beginning to fill with smoke. By then most passengers were out of their seats. A mass hysteria was sweeping through them. They were screaming, shoving and pushing to get to the doorways. Dusty felt herself being jolted rudely like a rag doll. Mack and the attendant struggled to get some order into the evacuation.

Outside, the winter gale drove slashing rain in sheets against the plane. Icicles were already forming along the edges of the downed jet. The howling wind whipped the evacuation slide, threatening to tear it from its brackets.

Within seconds, the passengers who could walk were sliding down in a steady stream, one after another, disappearing into the heavy rain below.

Dusty's instinct for survival told her to leap into the slide. The smoke was making her cough and she couldn't ignore the fact that the entire jet could explode into flame at any moment. But Mack did not make any move to leave the plane.

After the last person was down the slide, he hurried back through the plane to check on the source of the smoke while the flight attendants remained to take care of the injured who could not leave their seats.

At the moment Dusty did not have any particular desire to be a heroine. But how could she slide to safety when Mack was still on the plane with dozens of injured passengers?

Summoning her courage, she left the doorway and joined the flight attendants who were giving what first aid they could to the injured.

With the doors open, the smoke seemed to be lessening. Mack came back with the good news that the smoke had come from an electrical fire in the cabin, which the flight engineer had controlled with a fire extinguisher.

The second officer—the flight engineer—joined them and called Mack and Dusty and the four women flight attendants together in a huddle to assess the situation.

"It's beginning to look like the danger of fire is minimal. The heavy rain is washing away any fuel that might have spilled in the crash landing. So we're free from that danger, at least. But we're going to keep strict no-smoking regulations for the time being. How does the casualty list stack up among the passengers?"

"One elderly gentleman is having some symptoms of a heart attack," a stewardess said.

"A woman in my section appears to have some broken ribs. One man was thrown pretty hard against the side of the plane and has a dislocated shoulder, possibly a broken shoulder bone."

One by one, they listed the casualties. Five passengers in serious condition needed hospitalization and at least a dozen more were suffering from incapacitating injuries and shock. The first officer, who had piloted the craft down, was among the more seriously injured, and the captain had been blinded by flying glass and debris when the hijacker's bullet had smashed the front windshield.

"How soon will a rescue team get here?" one of the flight attendants asked the second officer.

He looked grave. "There's no telling. The hijacker put our radio out of commission when he took over so we were without air-to-ground communication long before the crash landing. I don't know how long we might have been tracked on radar."

"Won't they track us on the ELT now that we're down?" one of the uniformed women asked. The ELT—an emergency locater transmitter—sent out a constant beacon on a standard frequency that would lead other aircraft to the downed plane.

A frustrated expression crossed the engineer's face. "We suffered a lot of damage when we crashed into those rocks. It damaged the ELT. I'm going to try and patch it together but I don't know if I'll have any luck with it."

"Well," the senior flight attendant exclaimed, "if you don't think there's any danger of fire, the thing we have to do first of all is get those people out of the freezing rain and back into the plane for shelter as fast as we can, or we're going to have some cases of hypothermia to add to the casualty list."

With the plane tilted as it was, the crew decided to open the doors on the lower side and bring the passengers back in from that side. All the doors on the lower side, however, were jammed. Eventually they got one door open and soon the plane was filling up with shivering, wet people.

It was a miserable situation. There was no electricity, no heat. They were at an altitude of several thousand feet. Rain drummed steadily on the metal skin of the plane, coating it with ice. Flashes of lightning and crashes of thunder rumbled through the valleys and peaks of the high mountain range. It grew darker and colder inside the plane.

Wrapped in her trench coat, Dusty sat huddled near a window trying to keep warm as she stared out at the winter storm lashing at the wild and desolate mountains. With the passing of the first moments of tension following the crash, she had become aware of a dozen bruises. She wished miserably that she had a cigarette. Then she remembered that Mack had badgered her into quitting some time ago.

This wasn't the first tight spot she and Mack had escaped from since that first time she had laid eyes on him in the streets of Beirut. Then, like now, there had been a close brush with death.

That day in Beirut, she had been crouched near an overturned burning car. The street was cluttered with bricks and rubble from a bomb blast. She was oblivious to scattered gunfire in the area as she furiously snapped pictures of running, frightened people, some carrying the wounded.

Suddenly she was knocked flat. Later she likened it to being run over by a truck. She was smothered under bone-crushing weight. Then the weight lifted and powerful hands dragged her around the corner of a nearby building and into an alley.

When her stunned senses recovered, she twisted around and saw the rugged face of the big man hovering over her. "Are you out of your mind?" she gasped furiously.

She tried to sit up, but he pushed her back down.

She was on top of her camera, which she managed to drag from under her. "You idiot," she sputtered.

"Look what you've done. You've smashed a two-hundred-dollar lens."

Again she tried to sit up. When he made a second attempt to push her down, she fought him off. "Will you leave me alone?" she cried. "What kind of a nut are you, anyway?"

He nodded in the direction of the building across the street. "Machine gun," he drawled softly. "Guy in the window."

"Where?" Dusty gasped, raising her head to peek around the corner.

A loud clatter split the air. Bullets ricocheted off the sidewalk and walls.

"There," he answered laconically as she ducked back into the safety of the alley.

She hugged the wall and plunged her hand into her camera bag for another lens.

The man who had pulled her into the alley was sitting with his back against the brick wall. He was calmly eating what looked like a candy bar, which he'd taken from a pocket.

He fished another bar from his pocket and offered it to her. "Energy snack," he said. "Fruit, nuts and whole grains. Have one. It's good for you."

He was obviously an American. He was wearing scuffed boots, blue jeans and a worn corduroy jacket. There was something vaguely familiar about him.

Dusty ignored the fruit bar. She was still furious at him for manhandling her and breaking her favorite camera lens.

There was a pause in the shooting.

Dusty peered cautiously around the building. Fifty feet away, out in the street, were the remains of the overturned automobile. All that was left was a smoldering hulk of metal. She eyed the building across the street and the wrecked car, measuring her chances of getting to the shelter of the wrecked vehicle before the gunner in the building could reload.

"Damn!" she muttered recklessly. She drew a breath, her muscles tensing. Then she leapt to her feet and started running. Behind her she heard the American utter a surprised exclamation. She glanced back once, saw him take a stand in the mouth of the alley holding a heavy Colt .45 automatic in both hands. Then he fired rapidly at the building across the street. He was covering her!

"Thanks," she yelled as she made a slide to safety behind the car as if coming into home base after knocking a fly ball to center field. Instantly, she was on her knees, camera in hand. With its motor drive advancing several frames a second, she began filming the scene in the street, the frightened faces of men, women and children running or crouched behind any shelter they could find, the wounded sprawled in the gutter.

Across the street, the machine gunner had gotten a fresh clip in his weapon and began blazing away again. Dusty switched to a telephoto lens, raised her camera above the edge of the overturned car and snapped pictures of the machine gunner in the window. Bullets ricocheted off the pavement and smoldering metal. She hit the ground. From the alley, she heard the big American yelling some unprintable comments at her. She looked back, grinned and stuck her tongue out at him defiantly.

He gave her a disgusted look and drew back into the safety of the alley as he put a fresh clip in his automatic.

Just then an armored truck filled with Israeli soldiers appeared from around a corner. Dusty ducked again as more gunfire erupted. After a bit, she saw the soldiers pile out of the truck and scatter up and down the street. Obviously, they had taken care of the man with the automatic weapon. There was no more shooting.

Dusty slung her camera over her shoulder and cautiously moved away from the shelter of the wrecked car. Only then did she notice that the American who had pulled her into the alley was already striding down the block without giving her another glance. She watched his broad shoulders recede from sight, leaving her wondering who he was and where she had seen him before.

Most of the Americans she'd seen in this embattled section of the city were reporters or members of TV crews. But media people didn't go around armed with Colt automatics.

Dusty returned to her hotel. The place had a cosmopolitan atmosphere, filled with media people from all over the world.

The next morning on her way to the coffee shop, she stopped at the front desk to check for messages. The desk clerk handed her a sealed envelope with her name scrawled on the front. She tore it open. Inside, in the same heavy masculine scrawl, was a note: "Sorry about the camera lens." With the note were two one-hundred-dollar bills.

Dusty stared at the note and money with stunned surprise. "Who gave this to you?" she asked the clerk.

"I don't know his name."

"Big guy?" she prompted. "Six feet tall? Broad shoulders? American? Talks with a drawl?"

The clerk nodded.

"Is he a guest in the hotel?"

"I've seen him around here from time to time but he's not registered here."

She stuffed the envelope in her handbag and crossed the lobby to the coffee shop. There he was, seated alone at a table by a window, reading a newspaper as he ate breakfast.

Dusty felt a strange quickening of her pulse as she crossed the room to where he was sitting. "Hello," she said, loud enough to get his attention.

He glanced up from his newspaper.

"Remember me?"

"Sure I remember you," he said in his slow, drawling manner. "How are you this morning, Miss Landers?"

His voice sent a peculiar shiver down her spine. "Mind if I sit here?"

"Not at all." He rose and pulled a chair out for her.

"How did you know my name?" she asked.

"You're famous, aren't you, Dusty Landers? I've read quite a few of your articles. You're a good writer even if you haven't got much sense."

Her eyes widened and an angry flush stained her cheeks. "What is that supposed to mean?"

He took a sip of his fruit juice. "Anyone who takes chances the way you did yesterday couldn't have her head screwed on very tight."

Her eyes narrowed dangerously. "Listen, it's my business to take chances. Publishers don't pay big bucks for firsthand stories and pictures to journalists who sit home in rocking chairs."

He shrugged, not bothering to reply.

She was steamed. "I was going to give you the two hundred dollars back. After that crack, I think I'll keep it."

"Suit yourself."

"No, on second thought, I don't want anything from you." She took the two one-hundred-dollar bills from her handbag and flung them on the table beside his plate.

Thoughtfully, he picked them up. "Okay, if that's how you feel. I was responsible for breaking your lens."

"Well...I guess you meant well," she said, cooling down a bit. "You thought you were getting me out of a dangerous spot. And by the way—before you accuse somebody of not having her head screwed on tight—how about your John Wayne stand at the alley, blazing away at the sniper? Even if you were covering me, wasn't that just a shade foolhardy?"

He buttered his toast without replying.

She scrutinized him, intrigued and mystified. What was he doing in Beirut at a time like this?

A waiter appeared and she ordered her usual breakfast—a cup of black coffee. Then she directed her attention to the large man seated across the table from her. "So you know my name. Mind telling me who you are?"

"O'Shea. Mack O'Shea."

The name rang a bell. "Of course! I thought I'd seen you somewhere before. Mack O'Shea. The Dallas Cowboys. Five or six years ago. You played tackle. They called you 'the Slammer.' I read articles about you and saw some of the televised games you were in."

"That's ancient history."

"Then it's true. But what are you doing here, Mack O'Shea? This is no place for a football player."

"Retired football player," he corrected. "I only played those two seasons."

"I notice you avoided my question."

"Question?"

"Yeah. I was wondering what you're doing in a place like this. Pardon me for being nosy, but this is hardly a city for sightseers."

"I'm not vacationing, if that's what you mean. I have business interests here."

Somehow that did not satisfy her. American businessmen didn't carry pistols.

She was interrupted by the waiter bringing her coffee. She sipped it and lit a cigarette, taking a deep, satisfying drag.

O'Shea gave her an unbelieving look. "Is that all you're having for breakfast—a cup of coffee and a cigarette?"

"What do you mean? That's all I ever have for breakfast. It takes two cups of coffee and a couple of cigarettes to get my motor started in the morning."

He looked disgusted. "Breakfast is the most important meal of the day."

She frowned. "What are you—some kind of health nut?"

"I try to take care of myself, if that's what you mean. That's just good sense."

"So now you've appointed yourself my nutritionist. Yesterday you interfered with me doing my job. This morning you start out by telling me my brains are scrambled. Now you're trying to tell me what to eat for breakfast. Is there anything else? Do you want me to change my hairstyle? Maybe my makeup doesn't suit you."

He gave her a slow, thoughtful look, starting with her hair and ranging down her face to her breasts and back to her eyes. Her face grew hot at the male appraisal.

"No," he drawled. "That all checks out just fine. Too bad; at the rate you're living, it's not at all going to stay together."

"For your information I'm healthy as a horse."

"That's because you're so young. In a few years you'll be a wreck, the way you take care of yourself. But I wouldn't worry about it. You'll probably get shot full of holes long before that anyway."

"Aren't you the diplomatic one! Thanks for the vote of confidence."

He picked up his check. "If you want to ruin your lungs, that's your business. I don't want to sit around here ruining mine breathing your smoke. See you around."

"Not if I can help it," she flung after him.

She sat there fuming. What an insufferable dictator. Where did he get off criticizing her life-style? What lousy manners, to go around giving unsolicited advice!

She was so mad she had a second cigarette and another cup of coffee.

After a while some of the edge wore off her anger and she found herself reluctantly admitting that despite his rudeness, he was quite a male hulk in a rugged, battered sort of way. His clothes looked as if he'd slept in them and his shock of dark red hair defied her self-control; her fingers had itched to reach up and push back the curl that had fallen over his brow.

With an impatient gesture, she crumpled her cigarette in an ashtray and left the table.

For the rest of that day her mind was on things other than Mack O'Shea as she roamed the streets with her camera, taking the kind of close-up human-interest shots that would result in a powerful photo essay.

Back at the hotel that night, she bathed, changed from her jeans into a skirt and blouse and went down to the hotel restaurant for supper. When she entered the dining room, she saw a familiar head of dark red hair. Once again, Mack O'Shea was sitting at a table alone. This time she made it a point to select a table on the opposite side of the room.

She tried to avoid looking at O'Shea. There were more important things to occupy her thoughts. After dinner she would go up to her room and begin typing her article. As she ate, she planned the opening paragraph.

She was halfway through her salad when the room was shaken by a thunderous blast. Diners leapt to their feet, some of them crying out with alarm. The lights flickered. For a moment, Dusty was frozen in place. She heard an eerie, tortured whine, then another blast shook the building. Window glass shattered. Plaster from the ceiling came showering down. This time the lights went out, plunging the room into inky blackness.

Suddenly, a strong hand gripped her arm. She recognized Mack O'Shea's baritone voice. "Come on. We'd better get out of here."

"What's happening? Somebody set off a bomb?"

"More than that. We're getting shelled from some mortar batteries in the hills."

She didn't argue as Mack led her through the rubble and out into the street that was lit by the garish flicker of burning buildings. Another shell exploded a few blocks away, shaking the ground under her feet. She cowered against him, more frightened than she wanted to admit.

"What makes you think we'll be any better off out here in the street?"

"We won't be. But I know a place where we can go."

He led her across the street and then down a flight of stairs. He took out a small pocket flashlight that gave them some visibility in the inky blackness. They descended into a basement—some kind of utility annex with large generators and machinery.

Mack led her to a corner. "Might as well sit down and get as comfortable as possible. This shelling could go on for hours."

Dusty shivered in the chilling dampness of the underground chamber. "This reminds me of scenes from World War II movies. It's like an underground bomb shelter in London during the Blitz."

"Some things about wars don't change."

There was another earth-shaking reverberation as a shell exploded somewhere in the neighborhood. Dusty felt a clammy hand of fear clutching her throat. "I need a cigarette," she said desperately. To hell with Mack O'Shea and his aversion to tobacco. She would have lit up a cigarette if she had had one, but she'd left her handbag on the dining-room table.

"I have something better for your nerves—and your lungs," Mack said. He flashed his light on a bottle of wine he was carrying.

"Where did you get that?"

"Grabbed it up as I was leaving the table. Thought it might come in handy. Sorry I didn't bring glasses."

"I've drunk out of a bottle before."

Mack removed the cork, wiped the mouth of the bottle with his handkerchief and handed it to her.

Dusty took a swallow. "Not bad. You have good taste in wine." She tried it again, then passed the bottle back to him.

They settled down in the corner, leaning against the wall, passing the bottle back and forth.

"Have you noticed people always seem to be shooting at us?" Dusty observed.

"Must be the line of work we're in."

She didn't know if the wine was putting her in a mellow mood or if the situation had something to do with it, but her earlier anger toward Mack O'Shea seemed to have dissolved. At the moment she was glad to have the big Irishman at her side. His presence was somehow comforting. He appeared to know exactly what to do in a crisis. Later, looking back, she thought it was then that she first suspected he might be a CIA agent.

Her eyes were adjusting to the dim light enough to make out his features. "I hadn't really gotten started on my meal," she said. "I was halfway through my salad when that first shell exploded. Had you finished eating? I wonder if they'll charge us for the meal." She giggled. "That is, assuming the hotel is still there in the morning. Damn, I hope it is. All my camera equipment is in my room." She had another sip of the wine. "Have you been in Beirut long? This is my second week. I was going to finish up tomorrow and take the first flight I could get back to the States." She paused again. "You don't talk much, do you?"

He was leaning against the wall, looking at her with an amused expression. "Haven't had much chance," he drawled.

"I know. You can't get a word in edgewise. I talk a lot. Sorry. That's just the way I am. And getting scared out of my wits makes it worse and I guess the wine isn't helping any. You can blame yourself for that. You brought it. Myra—that's Myra Cox, my agent—says she doesn't know how I manage to get any decent interviews because I don't stop talking long enough for my subjects to say anything. Of course that isn't true. I don't rattle on like this when I'm interviewing somebody."

There was a short silence.

"Well, say something," Dusty said impatiently, "I stopped talking."

He chuckled. "Can't think of anything to say."

"The strong silent type, huh?"

"I wouldn't say that," he drawled.

There was another short silence before Dusty said, "Well, since it looks as if we'll be stuck here for the night we might as well get better acquainted. I've been trying to figure out your accent. It's southern, right? Not southwestern like Texas or New Mexico or Arizona, but not deep-south Carolina or Georgia, either."

"Are you a student of regional speech?"

"I get around a lot and I notice things like that. Can you tell where I'm from?"

"Definitely not New York or New England. Kind of western, I suppose, or midwest."

"That's pretty good," she said, somewhat surprised. She hadn't thought he was that observant. "I'm from Oklahoma, originally. Grew up in a little town not far from the reservation where my grandmother was born."

"Then you're part Indian."

She nodded. "My grandmother was a full-blooded Cherokee princess."

"That explains your dark hair and unusual skin coloring. And," he added with a chuckle, "your temper."

Her eyes narrowed. "Listen, I had a perfectly good reason to get mad at you. Of all the male, arrogant—"

She was interrupted by an earthshaking blast like a clap of thunder. She shuddered and without thinking about it moved closer to him. She forgot about being angry with him; it seemed pretty ridiculous to harbor feelings of resentment when they might die any minute.

"Well, I told you where I'm from. How about your background?"

"Louisiana," he said.

"See, I was pretty close. Southern, not southwestern. Cajun bayou country? No, I guess not. O'Shea is definitely not French."

"No, but I grew up with French-speaking playmates. By the time I started school I could speak Louisiana French as fluently as English."

"What was an Irishman doing in Louisiana?"

"My dad was in the oil business."

"Oh. Lots of money, huh?"

"I don't know what you mean by lots. We were comfortable."

"I'll bet you were. Compared to us you were probably rich. My dad had a gas station and store in a little crossroads town that had a cotton gin, a general store and a dance hall, and that was it. It was dusty in summer and cold as the North Pole in the winter. I had to ride a bus fifteen miles every day to school. It wasn't all that bad, though. I had a great family. I loved visiting my grandmother on the reservation. She was a very old lady and she told me wonderful stories by the hour. I learned all about the Indian culture and I know all the legends."

Mack listened, an expression of soft warmth in his eyes. "Bet you were a tomboy."

"What makes you say that?"

"Just guessing."

"Well, I suppose I was. I was sixteen before Mom could get me out of blue jeans and into a dress. I liked to go hunting and fishing with my brothers and ride horses." She grinned. "Once a kid in the sixth grade, Tommy Parkins, made some kind of insulting crack at me and I knocked him flat. Got expelled for a week for that."

Mack chuckled. "I'll bet you had a mean right hook."

"Just ask Tommy Parkins. How about you, Mack O'Shea? What was it like for you when you were growing up?"

"Oh, pretty routine. The usual—running around with friends, cramming for tests, sports. I was big on sports."

"I'll bet you were. Any big high-school romances?"

"I had a terrible crush on Miss Simpson, our tenth-grade math teacher."

Dusty laughed, forgetting for a moment the tension of their life-threatening situation. "Where did you go to college?"

"In Texas. TCU. My dad's alma mater."

"And you made all-American on the football team your senior year."

"How did you guess?"

"It figures. You went on to a pro-football career, didn't you?"

"Yeah. And how about you, Dusty? How did you get out of that little crossroads Oklahoma town with its general store, cotton gin, dance hall and your dad's filling station and turn into a globe-trotting photo-journalist?"

She shrugged. "I had a great English teacher in high school. He said I had writing talent. I was editor of the school paper and started taking pictures. I made good grades, got a college scholarship, earned a degree in journalism, worked on a local newspaper one summer, then began submitting articles to magazines. I sold some, moved to New York . . . and, well, here I am.''

"Looks like your high-school English teacher was right about your talent. Not many photojournalists get to be as successful as young as you are."

"I love it," she said simply. "It's my life."

She had another sip from his wine bottle. Not much more than an hour had passed since they'd ducked into this basement, but she felt as if she'd known Mack most of her life. She felt very comfortable with him. Her earlier resentment was forgotten completely. In its place had crept a warm feeling of companionship. They could possibly be sharing the last hours of their lives.

She tried not to think about that. She was sitting close to him, their backs resting against a wall. Her head settled onto his shoulder; it seemed a natural thing to do.

Presently, his arm slipped around her and drew her closer. She welcomed the warmth of his body. She felt secure in his embrace, less afraid and strangely vulnerable. For once in her life she didn't feel like talking. She wanted only to close her eyes and savor the good feelings.

He took her fingers in his big hand and kissed them one by one. She discovered that he could be surprisingly gentle for such a big, physical kind of man. "Dusty . . ." His voice sounded husky.

She looked up at him. Their eyes met and held. Their lips were very close. She could feel his breath on her cheek.

"This doesn't make sense," he said softly.

"I know," she murmured. She couldn't take her eyes from his.

"We've hardly known each other forty-eight hours, but . . . the way I feel . . ."

She said shakily, "I suppose it's the situation we're in . . . being scared together . . . the wine—"

"Do you really think that's it?"

"No," she admitted.

She'd heard there could be this kind of chemistry between a man and a woman, this kind of strong attraction.

Was that what was happening now? She didn't know, since she'd never felt like this before.

Mack's arm drew her closer. She raised her face to his, knowing he was going to kiss her. For a moment he delayed, a troubled expression in his eyes. Then, with a soft cry, his lips were on hers. Dusty expected to enjoy the kiss, but was unprepared for the raging flames it ignited.

Her whole body felt on fire, her nerve endings tingling from her head to her toes. Her breathing became strained as she returned his kiss hungrily, her fingers digging into his luxurious mop of hair. Forgotten was the shelling outside. Forgotten was everything except the raging desire that consumed her.

She gasped through parted lips as his kisses rained down her throat to her chest. His fingers fumbled with her blouse and then he found her breasts, full and aching for his lips. If this was insanity she never wanted to be sane again. Her defenses had been swept away. She was willing to be conquered here and now on this damp basement floor.

But Mack suddenly wrenched his lips from her with a broken cry. A shudder ran through the big man as he moved away and plowed shaking fingers through his hair.

She was frozen with shock. The beautiful moment was shattered. Dusty felt an icy chill quench the fires that had burned in her only moments before. Forlorn and betrayed, she sat apart from him, huddled and shivering.

"What . . . what's the matter?" she asked in a small voice.

"Dusty, I'm sorry," Mack O'Shea said in a voice that reflected his misery.

She closed her blouse with trembling fingers. "Sorry . . . ?"

"I had no right to start something like this. I . . . I got carried away. You're a very desirable woman. The two of us, alone like this . . . the situation. But that's no excuse."

"Maybe . . . you'd better explain," she said in a small, cold voice.

"I'm engaged to someone. Her name is Laura . . . Laura Nicholson. I've known her since we were in college. We're going to get married as soon as I get back to the States in a few weeks. I came very close to betraying her and hurting you."

Dusty felt as if a bucket of ice water had been dashed in her face. For once, she was speechless. She didn't know what she felt most, anger or hurt. "Thanks for getting around to telling me," she said cuttingly.

"I'm sorry."

Humiliation made her face burn as she thought about how close she had come to letting herself be seduced by this man. She'd behaved like a naive schoolgirl. As furious as she was with him, she was even more angry with herself. How could she have been so trusting, so willing, so easy? Normally, she was very cautious with men. They were always on the prowl, wanting everything and giving nothing in return. And here she'd been about to let herself be seduced by a man she'd known less than forty-eight hours...a stranger.

"Dusty, I really am sorry—"

"Oh, shut up!" She had drawn away from him, sitting in a small, cold huddle, her knees drawn up to her chin, her arms hugging her legs.

She refused to speak to him anymore. An hour passed in cold, strained silence. No more shells were exploding. When Mack said it was safe to leave the basement, they returned to the hotel. It had escaped any direct hits.

Dusty finished her work the following day and took the first flight she could get back to New York. She never wanted to lay eyes on Mack O'Shea again.

Putting him out of her mind was not that easy. He came back to her in her dreams. At unexpected times during the day, she would find herself shaken by the memory of that night and the passion his kisses had aroused. At times she hated him. Then she found herself defending him. Reluctantly, she had to admit that he had a streak of decency, for not wanting to betray his fiancée. He could very easily have been selfish and stolen a night's pleasure with Dusty. Given the opportunity, most men would have. But Mack O'Shea was that rare phenomenon—an honorable man. When she thought that way, she felt the hurt even more. She envied Laura Nicholson and wondered if Laura realized what a decent man she was getting.

Two weeks passed. She received a healthy-sized check for the Beirut story so she splurged on two expensive camera lenses and a portable lap computer she'd had her eye on for some time.

One day there was a knock at her apartment door. She looked through the peephole and saw Mack O'Shea standing there. She couldn't speak for a few seconds. "Go away!" she choked.

But he stubbornly kept knocking. Finally, she opened the series of security locks on her door.

"What do you want?" she demanded.

Mack looked at her for a long moment. In his soft, slow drawl, he said, "What I want is to marry you."

Mack found it was not easy to convince her. The argument went well into the night.

"You have to be out of your mind," Dusty said, pacing the room while she tried to hold back tears of anger and confusion. "We knew each other less than forty-eight hours in Beirut. How can you decide to do something this crazy?"

"It does seem crazy," Mack agreed in his slow, patient manner.

"I'm the one who does things on impulse, remember? You're the kind who plans everything."

"This isn't exactly an impulse," Mack replied. "I wouldn't go breaking an engagement on a whim. I haven't thought of much else for the past two weeks. I couldn't put you out of my mind, Dusty. I realized I'd never be able to forget you. I've known guys who have been married fifteen, twenty, thirty years. They start telling you about their lives. Somewhere in their past, there was a girl. They might have spent only one night with her, but she was something special. They didn't marry her for some reason. But they never forgot her. I thought about the look of regret that creeps into their eyes. I didn't want that to happen to me. Fifteen years from now, I don't want to think about that night you were in my arms in Beirut and get that look of regret in my eyes because I married somebody else.''

Dusty stared at him in amazement. This was the most she'd heard him speak at one time. ''How can you be so sure I'm all that special?'' she asked, feeling a catch in her throat.

''Well,'' he said thoughtfully, ''most of the day-to-day decisions we make are thought-out, rational judgments based on experience and information. But when it comes to some of life's biggest decisions, like a career or the person we want to marry, we have to rely on feelings that come from deep in our heart. They may not make complete sense to our rational level of thinking...they go a lot deeper than that—'' His gesture indicated an inability to explain more fully.

The argument went on over a dinner at an Italian restaurant in the neighborhood. Dusty knew she was licked. She'd known it the minute she'd opened her door and gazed at the big Irish lug with his mop of unruly russet hair and his rugged, less than handsome features. One look and she'd turned all soft inside. She, too, had known that she would never forget that night in his arms. It would forever occupy a secret part of her heart where bittersweet memories were stored.

She could think of a dozen perfectly logical reasons why she should not marry Mack O'Shea, but when he took her fingers in his big, clumsy hands and his blue eyes gazed at her as if she were the only other person in the universe, her rational thinking processes flew out the window.

She asked him about his fiancée. It had not been easy to call off the wedding, he told her soberly. "I care a great deal for Laura. We've known each other for years. We're almost like family. Her dad is like a second father to me. I wouldn't do anything to hurt her. But marrying her now would be incredibly hypocritical. It wouldn't be fair to any of us."

Mack O'Shea and Dusty Landers were married in New York before the week ended.

Chapter Four

It was not a typical marriage. Mack's undercover work was so secretive Dusty never knew where he might turn up. Her assignments took her to the far corners of the globe at a moment's notice. They ran up large telephone bills calling each other from halfway around the world, sometimes from primitive villages in third-world countries, other times from great cities like Rome or Amsterdam.

But when they were together, the sparks flew, igniting turbulent passions, making up for the separations. Electrical currents flowed. The chemistry was right. One look, one touch from him could arouse waves of desire.

Mack decided he was going to reform what he considered Dusty's vices. He launched a campaign to convince her to give up smoking and junk food.

"Get off my case, Mack O'Shea. Stop telling me what to do. You're not my father!"

"It wouldn't make any difference to me if I didn't care about you."

"I'm as healthy as a horse."

"Oh, yeah?"

"Yeah. Would you like for me to prove it on the tennis court this afternoon?"

"Is that a challenge?"

"What does it sound like?"

"Okay. Loser buys dinner."

She grinned. "If I lose, we eat at your health-food restaurant. If you lose, you buy me a milk shake and French fries."

Much to Mack's chagrin, Dusty proceeded to win. She was out of breath, but triumphant. "See?"

"Doesn't prove a thing," Mack grumbled. "You've still got youth on your side."

Though she'd never admit it to him, Dusty did secretly admire Mack for his healthy life-style. He was a marvelous physical specimen. She watched him work out at a gym, feeling a glow of pride and a quickening of her pulse at the sight of his powerful muscles bulging as he pressed heavy weights or pounded a punching bag.

She finally compromised. "All right; I'll give up cigarettes. But I'm keeping my junk food. If I have to kick the nicotine habit I'm going to need sugar and caffeine for consolation," she said stubbornly.

"Then take these."

"What are they?" she asked suspiciously.

"Vitamins."

"I am not going to go around gulping pills."

"They're not pills. They're a food supplement. The way you eat it's a wonder you don't get pellagra or beriberi."

She rolled her eyes heavenward. "Why of all the men on earth did I have to fall in love with a health nut? All right, gimme the bloomin' vitamins."

She took them when they were together to get him off her back, but as soon as she left on her next assignment, she forgot about them.

Any misgivings Dusty first had about the impetuous marriage had been swiftly dispelled. Mack was an exciting lover and a warm and considerate companion. In his arms, she found the complete fulfillment promised that night in the Beirut bomb shelter. She loved him intensely. When they were separated, a vital part of her was missing.

When they had fights, they soon patched things up, making love as passionately as they had argued. The lovers' quarrels reminded her of a line from a song she'd once heard: "lending a spice to the wooing."

Then, a few months ago, Mack dropped his bombshell.

"Dusty, I'm going to resign from my job with the CIA. All this cloak-and-dagger stuff used to be exciting, but I'm beginning to get tired of chasing all over the world. This isn't any way for us to have a family life. Robert Nicholson has offered me a good position with his oil company in Dallas. I'm seriously considering it."

Dusty was dumbfounded. She frowned, chewing her lip. "Robert Nicholson. Isn't he the father of your ex-fiancée?"

"What has that got to do with it?"

She wasn't sure. "Just wondering," she said, half teasing, half worried. She tried to keep her voice light. "She doesn't have something to do with this sudden decision, does she?"

"Of course not. Whatever gave you that idea?"

She shrugged. "You made an awfully hasty decision about breaking off your engagement with her to marry me. I just wondered if you might be having second thoughts."

"Of course not, Dusty. Don't be ridiculous. Anyway, this isn't a sudden decision. I've been thinking about it for some time."

"Well, anyway, I'm not sure I exactly like the idea of you working for her father's company while I'm off somewhere else."

"But you wouldn't be. That's the whole point, Dusty. I want both of us to stop this chasing all over the place. I don't know if you realize how much I worry about you. I know the kind of chances you take. Every time I see you off on a plane, I don't know if I'm going to see you alive again. This isn't any kind of a marriage. It's more of a legalized affair."

Dusty grinned. "I'm not complaining. At least you made an honest woman out of me."

But under her banter, Dusty was growing deeply disturbed. "Mack, what are you getting at? You aren't suggesting I give up my career, are you? I like what I'm doing."

"I don't expect you to become an ordinary housewife. I know what a fine photographer you are. But there are a lot of things you could do in Dallas—open a photography studio, take photos for an advertising agency, maybe publish a book of your work..."

Dusty made a wry face.

She had left the next day for London, profoundly upset. From the tone in Mack's voice, she knew he was dead serious about his plans. He'd brought up the subject of children. Of course she wanted children, but not for a few years. She couldn't very well start a family with the career she had now. "Mommy's going to be in Egypt next week. I'll phone from Cairo to tell you good-night." Some mother that would be!

She was all the more uneasy knowing how stubborn Mack could be. If he could only have waited a few more years!

He wouldn't let the matter drop. Their arguments became more and more bitter until the final explosion when she flew home from an assignment and found that Mack had moved out of their apartment. He said he'd done it hoping to shock her into seeing things his way. If that were true, it was an underhanded trick. Maybe it wasn't true! Maybe Mack's ex-fiancée was involved in their breakup. Maybe he was trying to make up his mind between the two of them.

That suspicion grew more convincing with each passing hour....

Suddenly her thoughts were interrupted as Mack sat down beside her. She became aware again of how uncomfortable it was in the downed plane. It was dark and cold. Freezing rain beat steadily against the metal skin and windows of the aircraft. The cabin, tilted at an angle, was cluttered with broken seats and luggage. The drumming of the rain mingled with moans from the injured passengers.

"How soon do you think we'll be found?" she asked anxiously.

Mack shook his head, looking worried. In a low voice he confided, "It doesn't look good. The ceiling is zero so we can't count on being spotted from the air. The ELT is beyond repair. Without that, the chances of searchers locating us in these mountains are zilch."

"Oh, Mack, we have some badly hurt people—"

"I know. We can't just sit here waiting for a search party to stumble on us. In this remote area, it could take days—weeks. I'm going to start hiking down the mountain. With some luck, I'll find a village."

"Good idea. I'm going with you."

"No, you're not."

She gathered up her camera bag. "Okay, then I'll go alone."

"Dusty, I forbid you to leave this plane."

She turned her jet-black eyes toward him with a look he knew all too well.

He sighed. "Listen to reason. For once stop being so blamed stubborn. We're in one of the most remote, rugged mountain regions in Mexico. The terrain is rocky and dangerous. With that rain freezing on the ground, we'll probably be scrambling down narrow trails covered with ice. One slip and you could fall a thousand feet. No telling what kind of wild animals we'd run into."

The look of determination in her eyes did not waver. "Number one," she said, "I'm as anxious as you are to get help to these people up here. Number two, I want to get my film to Myra while this story is breaking. So let's get going."

Mack looked frustrated and angry. Muttering, he rose and walked down the tilted aisle with Dusty close on his heels.

When Mack discussed his plans openly, several men volunteered to try the perilous journey, too, but Mack talked them out of it. He convinced them that he was better trained in survival skills.

To Dusty, he ordered, "You're to stick close to me."

She grinned. "Changed your mind, huh?"

"I know you well enough not to argue when you get that stubborn look in your eyes. You'd probably be blockheaded enough to start down the mountain by yourself. At least I can try to keep an eye on you." He thought for a moment, then added in a mutter, "Although with your temper, if you encountered a mountain lion, I'd feel sorry for the mountain lion."

She made a face at him, slung her camera bag over a shoulder and scrambled out the doorway.

A gust of icy rain pelted her when she dropped to the ground. She shivered, drawing her trench coat closer. This was definitely not going to be a pleasure jaunt.

It took no time for her to discover that Mack's description of the terrain was brutally accurate. They were above the timberline. The terrain was mostly barren except for small, stunted cedars and brush.

She slipped and fell repeatedly on the icy rocks, skinning her knees and hands. More than once, Mack's strong hand kept her from skidding over a ledge. Her lungs were straining in the thin air. The cold rain trickled inside the neck of her trench coat.

As night fell, the rain turned to sleet mixed with snow.

"We have to find some shelter for the night or we'll freeze," Mack said.

"Good idea," Dusty concurred through chattering teeth. "See a Holiday Inn anywhere?"

"No, but this looks like a cave," he replied, nodding toward a dark crevice between an outcropping of rocks.

He led the way over the rock-strewn terrain, approaching the cave entrance cautiously. "Let's see if it's occupied."

"Oc-occupied?"

"Yep. There's bears in these here hills," he drawled, taking a flashlight from his coat pocket.

Dusty felt a cold shiver down her spine, not from the icy rain this time. Her earlier bravado was beginning to desert her, though she was determined not to let Mack know that.

The beam from Mack's flashlight illuminated the shallow cave, showing it to be empty, much to her relief. She welcomed the dry shelter but she was wet and chilled to the bone, shivering uncontrollably.

"Have to get you warm and dry," Mack muttered, "or you'll get pneumonia."

"I saw plenty of dead cedar branches scattered around outside. They're wet, but there's some dry brush and sticks near the cave entrance. That's enough to get a good, hot fire started. Then we can feed the wet branches to it slowly. They'll dry out and start burning, too."

"Sounds like you've had some experience with camp fires."

"I went camping a lot with my brothers."

"Did your Cherokee grandmother teach you how Indians started fires by rubbing two sticks together? I brought some matches along, but they're wet."

Dusty reached in her waterproof camera bag and triumphantly produced a cigarette lighter.

Mack scowled. "Have you started smoking again?"

"It's a fourteen-karat-gold lighter. I couldn't bear to part with it."

"Well, for once I'm glad you smoked."

They gathered the dry brush into a pile. Dusty snapped her lighter and touched the flame to the brush, getting a flame started while Mack went outside to gather additional firewood.

Soon they had a fire blazing near the cave entrance. Still shivering hard, she spread her hands toward the welcome heat. She huddled near the fire, wanting to absorb the warmth into her chilled body. She could not remember when she had been so miserable. Besides being hungry, cold and exhausted, her morale was at an all-time low. They were lost somewhere in the wilds of these desolate Mexican mountains. It was entirely possible they were going to die here.

A wave of longing for the warmth and comfort of Mack's arms suddenly overwhelmed her. That only increased her sadness. Bittersweet memories of all the good times crowded her thoughts, blurring her eyes.

If only they could get back on good terms again. Well, she supposed they could if she'd give up her career. Glumly, she stared at the fire.

In the smoldering embers, she imagined she saw reflected episodes of her life like fragments of film clips—the little crossroads settlement that had been her home, her father's small, dusty store where he lived out his life, a kind, patient man who had long ago given up any dreams of being more than he was.

But she'd had her dreams. All the years she was growing up, she'd dreamed of the great world beyond the limits of the drab little community. She had devoured books and articles about the great cities, the foreign lands, the people, the events that shaped the world. She had read about presidents and generals and movie stars and scientists. There had been a hunger in her to see it all firsthand, to be a part of the events that made history. She didn't want to spend her life like her father, sitting it out on the sidelines.

Her brothers didn't have her kind of ambition. They were good, honest, decent men, but quite satisfied to earn a modest living and raise their families. Ted, the oldest, a truck driver, wanted no more from life than to one day own his rig free and clear. Billy, the youngest, helped her father in the store and eventually would take it over when her father started collecting his social security.

They had all been close when she was young, riding horses, hunting and fishing together. But as the years had passed, she had grown away from them, her ambition taking her through college on scholarships and student loans and eventually to New York. Now, when she visited them, they felt awkward with one another.

She remembered once, when she was a little girl, visiting her grandmother on the reservation; the old Indian woman had broken some sticks and had cast them on the ground. She had studied them carefully for a long time, then had said in her singsong way, "You will be the different one, my little child. The winds will take you far from here and you will see and do many things you do not dream of now.''

She had never forgotten her grandmother's prophecy.

Now Mack wanted her to put it all aside, to watch the great pageant of the world pass by while she stayed at home. It wasn't fair, she thought with a wave of rebellion.

Yet at the same time she harbored an inner conflict of guilt and the longing for children. It's not easy, she thought glumly, being a woman.

''You're going to have to get out of those wet clothes,'' Mack said gently.

His voice jerked her out of her reverie. Dusty glanced at him, frowning. She suddenly felt strangely self-conscious. ''I don't want to.''

''Why not, for heaven's sake? You'd prefer to get pneumonia?''

''Of course not,'' she said, trying to keep her teeth from chattering.

''Well, then?''

She was aware of him staring at her. In spite of the cold, she felt her face flush. ''I'm not going to undress in front of you, Mack O'Shea.''

He stared at her with an expression of disbelief. ''Why on earth not? I'm your husband.''

''I don't know if you are or not. I already made up my mind it was all over between us. I—I don't feel like we're married anymore.''

''It's just your stubbornness that has created this situation, Dusty.''

''Oh, yeah? I wasn't the one who packed up and moved out.''

"I explained my reason for that."

"I'm not sure I believe you. People who are happily married don't pack up and leave without talking things over."

"We talked this over for months. Talking wasn't getting us anywhere."

"Maybe that's because we have what the courts call irreconcilable differences."

"You didn't seem to have that attitude back on the plane when I was about to tackle that hijacker in the pilot's compartment. You looked at me like a woman in love."

She blushed. "Of course I care about you," she said angrily. "You can't live with a man for a long time without caring that he might get his head blown off in the next ten minutes. But that doesn't mean our problems have suddenly gone away."

Mack was becoming increasingly exasperated. "Dusty, this is no time for us to be discussing our marriage problems. You're sitting there soaked to the skin, half-frozen. So am I. It's not going to help either one of us to get sick. I've seen you running around nude a hundred times. I'm sorry this cave doesn't have a private boudoir to accommodate your sudden attack of modesty, but either you take those wet clothes off, or I'm going to take them off for you."

She glared at him. "You wouldn't dare, Mack O'Shea."

He glared back. "Want to bet?"

Her gaze held a moment longer, then she gave up with a sigh. This was one time she knew his determination was stronger than hers. She turned her back to him and began stripping the wet clothes from her cold body.

Not looking at Mack, she draped her sodden garments on stone outcroppings of the cave wall near the fire. Then she turned to the fire, grateful for the warmth.

Out of the corner of her eye, she saw that Mack had gathered a handful of dry moss from near the cave entrance. He grasped her arm firmly and began briskly rubbing it with the moss.

She tried to protest, but he held her firmly. "You have to get dry," he said.

Her protest grew weaker. A wave of pleasurable sensation spread through her. The moss brought glowing warmth to her skin. Her teeth stopped chattering. She felt the heat from the fire. The flickering light sent a ruddy glow over the cave walls and over her figure. She tried not to look at Mack, but it was impossible not to be aware of his sturdy physique so close to her side. As he dried her with the moss, she felt a different kind of heat, warming deep inside her, making her nerve ends tingle.

"That's—that's enough," she said unsteadily. "I'm dry now."

He tossed the moss in the fire where it exploded into soft, hissing sparks. He stared at the sparks, his eyes diverted from her. But she could sense his almost palpable need for her in the intimacy of the small cave.

Intuitively, she realized he, too, was filled with sadness and loneliness.

Something deep inside moved her to want to give him comfort. They both needed arms to hold them, the warmth of another being very close to give them shelter.

Almost shyly, she reached out her hand and found his. Their fingers entwined. She felt his grip tighten around hers. Then his big, strong hands moved to her neck, giving her a gentle massage, starting at her neck and moving down her back.

"Mack, stop that," she said weakly.

"Sure you want me to?"

"Yes," she said without conviction.

"You're very tense."

"Well, you aren't helping matters any."

"Why not? You always liked it when I massaged your back. You said it relaxed you."

"This is different and you know it."

"It is?"

"Yes, of course...."

Her voice had grown thicker. Her legs felt weak. "Mack, you're not being fair. Please stop that."

His large hands closed around her shoulders and he drew her to him. He murmured her name huskily. "Dusty..."

She pulled away from him, her quivering breasts rising and falling. "Mack, if—if we do it...if we make love, it won't solve a thing. It won't make our differences go away. Afterward, we'll still have the same problem that's tearing us apart."

Mack seemed at a loss for a reply. Agonized longing blazed in his eyes. It melted her heart.

Instead of any further words, Mack roughly drew her closer. His arms became tight bands around her. Her breasts were mashed against his broad chest. The sensation of his bare flesh against her awoke in her a throbbing wave of desire. Her breath became a rasping gasp. As if having a will of their own, her arms encircled his neck and she joined his effort to press their bodies even closer. His name became a choked moan on her trembling lips.

It was no longer a matter of his overcoming her resistance. There was no conquest, no surrender. There were no victors or conquered. She simply no longer had the strength or will to resist his need or her own.

Instead, she let herself be swept into the tidal wave of emotional hunger that was engulfing them both and joined him in the eager search for pleasurable sensations. Their hands and lips were touching, caressing, kissing.

Dusty was vaguely aware of the ruddy light from the camp fire flickering over their embracing bodies. She felt the pressure of his muscular thighs against hers, the hard ridges of his stomach against her soft belly.

Mack scooped her up in his powerful arms and gently laid her on a bed of moss beside the fire. Their exclamations mingled with the hissing, crackling sound of the fire. Outside, the wind moaned through the scrubby cedars and frozen boulders but in the small, sheltered cave it was snug and cozy. Their lovemaking rustled the bed of moss. They were fiercely demanding of one another, reaching for a spiraling, exquisite fulfillment.

At last, Dusty lay exhausted and content in the circle of Mack's arms. Her fingers traced the outline of his profile: his nose, his lips, his chin, down to the scar on one broad shoulder where he'd caught a bullet in an ambush one night in Central America, and then to the wiry curls of hair on his chest. The journey her fingers took, exploring intimately the muscles and sinew of his powerful physique, sent a delicious shiver through her body.

Gradually, as the tidal wave of passion subsided, cold reality returned and with it a wave of sadness.

She sighed. "Mack, why do you have to be so pigheaded?"

"Pigheaded?"

"You know good and well what I mean. We got along fine before you got this unreasonable notion of forcing me to give up my career."

"It's not unreasonable. It's a mature decision. There are certain responsibilities that go with marriage and raising a family. You're refusing to accept those responsibilities. You want to go on with this juvenile chasing all over the globe. I feel like I've got a shadow for a wife. I want a real flesh-and-blood woman I can come home to every night, who will help me establish a home and raise a family."

She blinked back tears, and turned away from him. Just as she had prophesied, nothing had changed. Tonight's intimacy had only made the heartbreak worse. She clenched her fists, determined it would never happen again.

Chapter Five

After a while, Dusty checked her clothes and found them dry. She dressed and lay down by the fire again. She slept fitfully, waking at times to see Mack stirring the embers of their camp fire and adding new branches.

At dawn, they ate sandwiches Mack had brought from the plane and then resumed their hike down the mountain. During the night, the rain had turned to snow. Now the sky had cleared to a brilliant blue and the sun sparkled on the snow and ice.

They walked in silence, not wasting breath on words. That suited Dusty; she didn't want to talk to Mack this morning. By noon they were below the timberline. It became warmer and easier to breathe. The snow had not reached this lower elevation.

Suddenly, Mack uttered an exclamation and pointed to tracks ahead of them. "We're getting close to some kind of civilization. Those tracks were made by horses."

Dusty felt a surge of relief. But then her joy dampened. "Maybe they're wild horses."

Mack knelt to study the tracks. "No, these were made by shod horses. We may be near a ranch of some kind."

They had another sandwich to celebrate, then began walking again, following the tracks. Dusty's strides had lightened with the joy of knowing they would soon find people who could help them. She strained her eyes eagerly, searching the area ahead to catch the first glimpse of civilization.

Suddenly there was a rustling in the brush. Dusty spun around. Two men on horseback seemed to have materialized out of thin air.

Dusty uttered a happy shout and ran toward them. Mack followed a bit more cautiously, carefully scrutinizing the two men. One of them was tall and thin, his face pitted with pockmarks. The other had a scar running from his ear down his cheek to his chin.

Dusty was talking a mile a minute when Mack reached her side. The two men were staring at her blankly.

"Dusty, I don't think they understand English," Mack said. he addressed them in fluent Spanish.

Dusty knew enough Spanish to understand he was telling them they were lost and needed to get to a telephone.

"Tell them about the plane," she prompted.

But Mack ignored her. The two men had directed their attention to Mack. Finally the one with the pitted face spoke briefly, saying to follow them. He took the lead. His companion trailed behind them.

"I don't like the looks of this," Mack muttered.

"What do you mean?"

"Those two hombres are armed."

Dusty had seen the pistols in holsters on their belts. "Don't ranchers often carry guns on account of snakes and things?"

"Those two don't look like ranch hands to me. Look at those fancy saddles—hand-tooled with silver inlays. Must have cost a fortune. And those boots and hats don't look like the kind working men wear."

She frowned uneasily. "Do you think they're criminals?"

"No telling, in a remote region like this. They could be bandits or drug traffickers."

"Oh, great," she muttered glumly.

"I hope I'm wrong."

"I hope so, too," she said, but not with much conviction. Mack's CIA training had given him a sixth sense about things like this.

They walked steadily for nearly an hour. The horsemen said nothing more to them. One led the way while the other stayed behind them. Dusty had the apprehensive feeling that they were already prisoners.

The trail they were following became level. They emerged from the woods into a secluded valley surrounded by towering, snowcapped mountains. The sky, swept clear of last night's storm, was a brilliant blue. The mountain air was crisp. Under other circumstances, she would have found the scenery breathtaking, but she was too worried to be sight-seeing.

The trail led to what appeared to be a small ranch. There was a corral containing horses and a cluster of adobe and frame buildings.

Dusty's spirits brightened a bit. "You and your suspicious nature," she grumbled to Mack. "They're ranchers."

"Hope you're right," was his only reply.

The two horsemen dismounted, tied their reins to a hitching rail and motioned for Mack and Dusty to follow them into what appeared to be the main ranch house, a low, rambling structure constructed of unpainted lumber.

From the main hallway, they passed through a doorway into a room furnished with rough, hand-made furniture, hide-bottomed chairs and a lumpy couch. Hung on the unpainted board walls were buck horns, a coiled lariat and several bullfight posters. Along one wall was a rack containing enough rifles and shotguns to start a small war.

She took it all in with a glance and then her attention centered on the room's occupant, a huge, swarthy man with a drooping mustache who was seated at a table, noisily devouring a plate of enchiladas. He wore boots, an ornate holster filled with a big, silver revolver and a cartridge belt across his shoulder, Pancho Villa style.

In his presence, the two men took off their hats and addressed him with respect, speaking in rapid Spanish. Dusty caught enough words to make out that they were telling him how they had stumbled on her and Mack up in the mountains this morning. The big man apparently ran the place. He was addressed as *jefe*, the Spanish word for "chief" or "leader."

He grunted, sucked the enchilada juice from his fingers and leaned back in his chair, scrutinizing Dusty and Mack with eyes that glittered under bushy eyebrows. A Western-style hat was pushed back from his perspiring forehead.

He said in perfect English. "Welcome to our humble hacienda, my friends. *Mi casa es su casa*. Permit me to introduce myself. I am José Guzmán."

"How do you do," Mack said slowly, his voice and eyes guarded. "I am Mack O'Shea, and this is my wife."

José Guzmán bowed. "You are to be congratulated, sir, on having such a beautiful wife." The compliment did not alleviate the uncomfortable shiver that ran down Dusty's spine at the man's stare.

Then he asked, "May I ask what two *Americanos* were doing wandering around in these mountains?"

Before Dusty could say anything, Mack replied, "We wandered off from our camp and got lost. Perhaps you have a telephone we could use?"

The burly man picked at a tooth with his little finger. "Perhaps. You were camping, you say?"

"Yes."

Dusty thought it best to keep her mouth shut for once. There was an uncomfortable tension in the room. She instinctively sensed that Mack O'Shea and José Guzmán were two men not unfamiliar with violence who were sizing up one another.

"This is not a place where *norte-americanos* very often come for camping trips. There are others in your party?"

Mack was silent for a moment, then replied. "Yes. Since we did not return to camp last night, they'll no doubt be on their way to town to notify the authorities."

Guzmán's dark eyes seemed to glitter more brightly. "What town is that, *Señor*?"

Mack shrugged. "I can't pronounce the names of these Mexican towns."

"Hmm. 'Chula Vista' is not so difficult to say, *señor*."

Mack did not reply. *Well, you blew that one, Mack O'Shea,* Dusty thought.

There was a moment of silence. José Guzmán appeared to be turning this situation over in his mind. He snapped an order to his men. They moved swiftly. One grabbed Dusty's camera case. "Hey!" she said furiously, but he wrenched it from her hand. The other quickly searched Mack, found the hijacker's pistol in his belt under his coat. They placed the gun and camera case on the table in front of Guzmán.

He picked up the heavy pistol and turned it over in his hands. "A .357 Magnum. Quite a powerful weapon for a tourist, *señor*."

Mack said nothing.

When the large man behind the table opened Dusty's camera case, she could no longer keep quiet. "Get your mitts off my cameras!" she cried furiously. She took a step toward the table but one of the men grabbed her arm, forcing her back.

Guzmán removed the cameras and lenses, murmuring to himself as he examined them. "Very professional equipment, *señora*."

He put the cameras back in the bag, then leaned back in his tilted chair, propping his boots on the table. "Well, *señor* and *señora*, I tell you what I think. I think you are government people from the United States, CIA, perhaps, sent to spy on ranchers like us to see if we are raising marijuana."

Boy, that's ironic, Dusty thought. Mack had worked for the CIA but he'd resigned. He really was a civilian!

"You are quite mistaken, *señor*," Mack said. "We're just tourists, like I told you. If we were with the CIA, that should not bother an honest rancher like yourself."

Honest rancher, my eye, Dusty thought grimly.

José Guzmán scowled. He said nothing for a minute or two, apparently wrestling with the situation. Finally he spoke. "You will be our guests until I can check out this matter." He signaled to the two men who had brought them, then resumed his meal, indicating that the interview was concluded.

The pockmarked one prodded Dusty, nodding toward the door. "Wait a minute," she exclaimed, "I'm not leaving without my cameras."

The man guarding her gave her a shove. Angrily, she spun to face him, a torrent of hot words on her lips. But Mack was giving her a stern look. "Dusty...drop it."

She was not in the mood to drop anything. But the look in Mack's eyes made her hesitate. With a supreme effort, she throttled her temper for the time being and proceeded to the door, muttering under her breath.

They were led from the main house across the yard to an adobe building. There they were escorted into a room where their guards left them, closing the door.

Dusty took in her surroundings. The room contained a bed, a table and some chairs of the same rough, hand-made style she'd seen in the main ranch house.

Then her gaze moved to the room's single window and a chill went down her spine. There were heavy bars made of strong oak spokes on the window. She tried the door knob. It was locked.

"We're prisoners!" she gasped.

"Looks like it," Mack agreed.

"Well, you don't seem very concerned!"

"Not much we can do about it," he replied laconically.

"Well, at least you could act a little more upset! Who are these people? What right have they got to lock us up?"

Mack went to the window and rested his arm on the sill as he surveyed the yard. Finally, he drawled, "Whatever they are, I don't much think they're honest ranchers."

Still furious over the loss of her cameras, she directed her anger at Mack. "Oh, you figured that out, did you?"

Ignoring her sarcasm, he continued in his slow, thoughtful manner. "Could be raising a crop of marijuana. Lot of that going on in these remote areas. They harvest the stuff, then fly it across the border. Or they could just be old-fashioned renegades and bandits."

Before Dusty could reply, there was the sound of the door being unlocked. A woman entered, carrying a tray of food covered with a cloth. She placed it on the table and left without saying a word. Dusty heard the lock click behind her.

Dusty removed the cloth. There were dishes filled with generous servings of tamales, enchiladas, steaming tortillas and guacamole plus some bottles of cold Mexican beer.

"Well, at least they're not planning to starve us to death," Dusty observed.

"Good, I'm hungry enough to eat a horse."

Mack took a seat at the table.

Dusty stared at him with an incredulous expression. "You're just going to sit there and calmly eat lunch while they steal my cameras and make prisoners out of us?"

"What would you suggest I do?" Mack asked, sampling the tamales.

"I don't know—something. What do you CIA types do in a situation like this?"

"Well, if we're served a great meal like this, we enjoy it."

"Can't you bust down the door or pick the lock or overpower the guards or something? Didn't they teach you stuff like that in the CIA?"

"You've seen too many James Bond movies. Hey, you ought to taste these enchiladas. They're great. Very nutritious, too. Lots of protein and there's natural grain in the corn tortillas."

"Don't you ever eat anything just because it tastes good?"

"You're just peeved because they stole your cameras."

"You better believe I am! It isn't only the cameras. All the shots I took of the hijacking are in that camera bag. Why didn't you tell them about the plane crash, by the way?"

"And have them find the plane and rob everyone on it?"

"Yeah, I guess you used your head there," she admitted.

The delicious aroma of the spicy food was getting to her. She took a seat at the table, removed the corn shuck from a tamale and took a tentative taste. "This is good," she admitted. She suddenly realized how hungry she was. The room became silent for a while as they both ate.

After the meal, Mack stretched, patted his stomach contentedly and lay down on the bed.

Dusty gave him a disgusted look. "Fat lot of good it does me to get locked up with an ex-CIA agent. All you seem to know how to do is eat and sleep. It's a wonder the CIA didn't fire you."

"In a situation like this, it's a good idea to conserve your energy," he murmured sleepily. "You can sit around fretting and stewing if you want to. I didn't get much sleep last night in that cave."

Dusty paced the length of the room several times, occasionally pausing in exasperation as Mack drifted peacefully off to sleep.

It occurred to her that after the sleepless night and the long hike down the mountain she, too, was exhausted. She gave up fighting off her fatigue and eased down on the bed beside Mack. Her head hardly touched the pillow before she was sound asleep.

She had wild dreams that she was riding with a band of Mexicans fighting a revolution. They wore cartridge belts over their shoulders and looked like José Guzmán. A man on a big white horse came riding out of the hills and captured her and he turned out to be Mack dressed in a big sombrero and the white pajamalike garb of a peon revolutionary.

He had her by the shoulders and was shaking her. Then she became aware that Mack really was sitting on the side of the bed, gently shaking her awake.

She blinked several times and groggily looked around. To her surprise she saw that night had fallen. It seemed that she had barely closed her eyes, but she must have been asleep for hours. The room was illuminated by the soft yellow glow of a kerosene lamp.

"Hi, feel better?" Mack asked.

"I guess so...."

"I want you to do something for me."

"Does it have anything to do with busting out of this joint?"

"Matter of fact, it does."

She sat up, coming fully awake. "Well, it's about time. What do you want me to do?"

"Stand over there and keep your ear against the door. Let me know if you hear anybody coming."

"What are you going to do?"

"Saw through a couple of bars."

"How do you plan to do that?"

"I'll show you."

He stripped his belt from the waistband of his trousers. Turning it over, he opened a small flap and withdrew what looked like a piece of steel wire about eighteen inches long.

"What's that?" Dusty asked curiously.

"One of the gadgets I carried with me when I was with the CIA. Useful little tool. Never know when one of these will come in handy. Glad I bought one for my own use."

"What is it?"

"Pocket saw. Flexible steel wire with a rough finish that will cut through wood or plastic. Probably wouldn't do much against steel bars, but it looks like they made the bars on the window out of wagon-wheel spokes."

"Hey, that's neat!" Dusty exclaimed. "I take back all the mean things I said about you and the CIA."

Dusty hurried to the door. Mack put one end of his wire saw around the bar, grasped both ends firmly and drew it back and forth in a swift, sawing motion. Dusty felt a surge of elation as he cut into the wood.

Suddenly her ears picked up the sound of heavy footsteps outside the door, then a key grating in the lock. She made a frantic warning motion to Mack who immediately stepped back from the window and shoved his wire saw into a pocket.

Not a moment too soon. The door swung open and one of their captors, the one with the jagged scar down one side of his face, entered the room.

He glanced at Mack, then directed his attention to Dusty. "You come. Señor Guzmán want talk you."

Dusty gave Mack a stricken look. He nodded slightly. She didn't like it, but she had little choice. Apprehensively, she moved ahead of the scar-faced guard. He locked the door then directed her across the yard to the main ranch house. There they again entered the room that appeared to be the headquarters of the renegades' leader.

José Guzmán was standing near a window puffing on a large cigar. He turned when they entered, his glittering dark eyes drinking in the sight of Dusty in a way that made her skin crawl. He gave Scar Face a curt order, dismissing him. Then Dusty was alone with the bandit leader.

Guzmán had changed into a shirt with decorative stitching and gleaming silver buttons. His boots were polished to a brilliant sheen. Around his waist was an ornate gun belt that held a matched pair of silver pistols with ivory grips. An enormous diamond sparkled on one finger of his left hand. His long mustache had been waxed, every hair in place.

He gave her a sweeping bow. "*Señora*, you do me a great honor to pay me this visit."

"Yeah, well, I didn't have much choice," Dusty muttered.

"Our ranch is very isolated," Guzmán continued. "It is not often I have the pleasure of entertaining a beautiful woman. Would you care for a drink?" He strode to a liquor cabinet. The sound of squeaking leather accompanied his movements.

Dusty swallowed hard. "I'm—I'm not really thirsty."

"But, please. You must taste this. It is very fine brandy from Monterrey."

He handed her a glass. He was standing closer to her now and had not taken his eyes off her since she'd entered the room.

Dusty took a swallow, coughed and blinked rapidly. She was growing more nervous by the moment. The look in Guzmán's eyes resembled a wolf eyeing its prey.

She backed away from him. "That's—that's real good brandy. I don't drink brandy very much. In fact I don't drink at all very much. I had an uncle who drank a whole lot. Uncle Clem. He was a real souse. Kind of the family drunk, you know. But I just have a social drink now and then. Mack, my husband, says that's at least one vice I don't have. He's always getting on me about the way I eat. He says I drink too much coffee and smoke too many cigarettes. Well, I did, that is. Smoke too many cigarettes, I mean. But I don't anymore. I finally managed to quit. It was tough, but he kept after me about it and I really am glad he did. You know, all the business about lung cancer and everything. Did you know that women are starting to get it as much as men now? Of course there are times that I miss it. Like right now, I'd really like to have a cigarette. That's a very pretty ring you have...."

Guzmán was staring at her, his mouth slightly agape. "*Señora*, you have a lovely voice, but you talk a great deal."

"Yes, I know. I talk too much. That's another bad habit I have. Mack, my husband, doesn't talk a lot, but I'm always rattling on, especially when I get nervous. I don't know how he puts up with me rattling on the way I do. Sometimes I guess he wishes I'd run down. I really can't blame him, but—"

"*¡Cállate!* Shut up, woman!" he thundered. "*¡Madre de Dios!* Don't you ever stop talking?"

She was moving backward as José Guzmán continued relentlessly to come closer until he had her backed into a corner. His face was flushed; his eyes were gleaming hungrily as his gaze trailed from her lips down her throat to her breasts.

Then his voice dropped to a purr. "*Señora*, you are the most desirable woman I have ever seen. Your skin is like the petal of a flower. Your hair is silk, your eyes are beautiful dark pools...."

Dusty managed to extricate herself from the corner and began her retreat around the room again. "I bet you say that to all the girls. I know all about you Latin types, how you like to flatter women...part of the macho image—"

Guzmán was breathing harder. His voice had grown thick with passion. Impatiently, he reached out and caught her arms. "*Señora*, I am burning inside. You have set me afire. I will have you. Do you understand? Fight if you wish. It will only give me more pleasure...."

Dusty's heart was pounding. It seemed to be sending ice water instead of blood through her body; she was shivering with fright and anger. She struggled to wrench her arms free from Guzmán's grasp, but her struggling only inflamed him more.

Suddenly Guzmán froze. He was staring past Dusty's shoulder. A strange, sick expression crossed Guzmán's face and he turned a pasty gray. His hands became sweaty and he dropped her arms.

Dusty spun around.

Mack was standing in the doorway holding a double-barreled shotgun.

With lightning speed, she moved out of Guzmán's reach. He glared at her, realizing he'd lost his opportunity to hold her as a shield as Dusty ran to Mack's side. "How did you do it?" she gasped.

"Finished sawing the board. Caught a guard napping." Then to Guzmán, he ordered, "Drop the gun belt."

Guzmán's face was black with fury. His fingers trembling with impotent rage, he unbuckled the gun belt. Heavy with the two pistols, it fell to the floor with a thud.

"Now," Mack said, "drop your pants."

Guzmán's eyes widened incredulously. "What?"

Mack waved the shotgun menacingly. "You heard me."

Swearing eloquently in Spanish, Guzmán reluctantly obeyed.

"Now go over to that chair."

Dusty laughed at the sight of José Guzmán in dingy underwear, his pants down around his ankles as he hobbled to the chair.

"Dusty, there's some rope over in the corner. Tie him up."

Guzmán gave Mack a cold, deadly stare. "*Señor*, you will never get out of these mountains alive. My men will track you down and I will see that you die a very slow and painful death."

"Dusty, I'm getting tired of listening to him. Stuff something in his mouth."

She found some rags and cut off Guzmán's torrent of Spanish expletives with a gag.

Mack checked the rope that bound Guzmán to the chair. Satisfied with the knots, he said, "All right, Dusty, let's get the hell out of here."

"Wait a minute."

She started jerking open closet doors.

"Just what do you think you're doing?"

"Looking for my camera bag."

"Dusty, damn it, we haven't got time for that. The guard I knocked out will be waking up any minute. He'll have the whole den of thieves down on us."

"I'm not leaving without it," she said stubbornly.

Mack glared at her. Then he took her cigarette lighter out of his shirt pocket and tossed it to her. "Here. Light that and hold it under one of Guzmán's feet. Maybe he'll tell you."

Dusty looked at the bandit leader, who was staring at the lighter and sweating profusely. "You think I won't do it?" she threatened.

Guzmán nodded vigorously in the direction of a cabinet across the room. She went to it, pulled out a drawer, then another.

"Dusty, hurry," Mack said urgently. "We're gonna be sitting ducks—"

"Here it is!" she cried. She caressed the familiar worn leather surface, then opened the bag.

"Now what are you doing?" Mack demanded.

She snapped a small electronic flash onto one of the cameras. "I'm not going to miss this." She pointed the camera at Guzmán, who glared murderously at her with bulging eyes, choking behind his gag.

"Dusty, you're going to get us killed!" Mack said furiously.

The flash went off. Then she dropped the camera in her bag and slung it over a shoulder. "Okay, let's go."

"Grab Guzmán's pistols and come on!"

Carrying a heavy six-shooter in each hand, she ran out of the building at Mack's heels.

"There are three vehicles in the yard," Mack said in a low voice. "A Jeep and two pickups. I vote for taking the Jeep. It's the newest of the three." Then he nodded toward another building, from which emanated the sound of voices and Mexican music. "I think the boys are whooping it up. If that guard I clobbered doesn't come around, we should be able to drive out of here without being seen."

"Do you think he'll wake up?" she whispered nervously.

"Well, I hit him pretty hard."

He paused beside one of the trucks, eased up the hood and ducked his head under it.

"What are you doing? I thought we were taking the Jeep."

He emerged from under the hood, holding something. "Rotor out of the distributor," he said. "Can't start the truck without it. I don't want to be chased."

He performed a similar operation on the other truck. Then they got in the Jeep.

"No keys," Dusty said, her heart sinking.

"No problem."

This time he ducked under the dash and tied some wires together. The engine turned over and started.

"Did you learn how to hot-wire cars in the CIA?"

"No, I picked that up in high school."

He threw the vehicle into gear. As the engine thundered and the rear wheels spun, Dusty was thrown against the seat.

"Hang on!" Mack yelled.

They roared out of the yard in a cloud of dust.

Dusty clung to the seat for dear life as the four-wheel-drive vehicle bounced violently. She heard a chorus of yells behind them.

"I think the guard came to," she cried over the clatter of the engine.

"They'll never catch us on horseback."

They were swerving and jouncing down a rough dirt road. The wind whipped her hair around her face. She realized she still had Guzmán's pearl-handled six-shooters.

"Can I shoot one of these off?"

"Do you know how?"

"Are you kidding? I told you I grew up in the Oklahoma countryside with two brothers. They had me rabbit hunting before I could spell my name."

"Go ahead, then."

She pointed one of the pistols at the sky and pulled the trigger. There was an ear-splitting blast as the heavy gun kicked in her hand.

"Yahoo!" she yelled at the top of her lungs.

Chapter Six

They bounced down the rutted dirt road, slamming around hairpin turns and giant boulders, sometimes skirting sheer drops down the mountainside. Dusty held on for dear life, trying not to scream.

"Slow down, for crying out loud," she gasped.

But Mack continued to drive at breakneck speed. "We have to get help up to those people in the plane as soon as possible."

More than once they got lost in the inky darkness and the maze of crisscrossing primitive mountain roads. It was dawn when at last, to her joy, Dusty saw the lights of a village in a valley below.

It was the town of Chula Vista, which José Guzmán had mentioned—a cluster of one-story adobe dwellings around a dusty square. The largest building in the village was a cathedral, its steeple and cross outlined against the pink dawn sky.

Roosters crowed vigorously as they entered the outskirts of the village. Dogs ran after the Jeep, barking. People came out of their adobe dwellings and stood in their yards to stare at them.

"Finding a telephone in a remote village like this is going to be a problem," Mack said.

"How about the priest at the cathedral?"

"Good idea. He'd know if anyone would."

Mack drove the dusty Jeep into the churchyard. Next door was a building that looked like the rectory. They knocked on the door and eventually a sleepy, bald-headed priest in a bathrobe opened the door.

Mack spoke quickly in Spanish, explaining who they were. He described the situation with the downed jet airliner and emphasized the urgent need to find a telephone.

The priest's eyes widened and he came fully awake. He hurried to dress, then accompanied Dusty and Mack to the home of the town's mayor. There was another exchange of excited Spanish and Mack was escorted to the mayor's telephone. The priest and mayor watched as Mack used the telephone. It didn't take him long to reach the proper authorities.

"The federal highway police will have a helicopter here very quickly," Mack told them.

"A helicopter? Here?" the mayor said in awe. *"Madre de Dios."* He crossed himself.

News of the event spread like wildfire through the village. By the time the helicopter, its blades whipping up a cloud of dust, landed at the town square, it was surrounded by a throng of wide-eyed villagers and barking dogs.

Dusty was busy with her camera, grabbing human-interest shots of the awe-filled faces; most of the people had never seen a helicopter before.

The pilot switched off his engine and swung to the ground to greet Mack and Dusty. He told them that rescue teams and helicopters had been combing the mountains without success since the jumbo jet vanished. "Nobody has known where to look," he said. "They lost all radar and radio contact with the plane. It was assumed beyond a doubt that the craft had gone down, but no one could pinpoint where."

"Well, we can show you," Mack said. "Let's get going. There are people up there urgently in need of medical help."

Mack and Dusty took seats in the helicopter. It took off, the giant blades biting into the clear, cold mountain air. Over the din, Mack shouted directions to the pilot.

With Mack's guidance, they were able to spot the downed airliner in the mountain wilderness. It was obvious to Dusty that searchers might never have located the airliner if she and Mack hadn't gone for help. The plateau was nestled among mountaintops shrouded in mist. With nothing to guide them, searchers could only guess where the jet could have vanished in the vast Sierra Madres.

The helicopter pilot radioed the location before attempting a landing. He circled the area until they were joined by more helicopters.

Then the airlift got underway.

When the helicopters landed near the jumbo jet, they were greeted with cries of joy. Dusty jumped to the ground, ducking under the wind whipped up by the copter blades. A woman flight attendant ran to her, sobbing. "We'd almost given up," she choked. "Some of those poor people...they're suffering so."

Dusty helped rescuers lower the more seriously injured from the jet on stretchers. When she had the opportunity, she was busy with her camera, freezing the dramatic moments on film. With a pocket recorder, she taped interviews with some of the hijack victims and with one of the handcuffed hijackers, who was willing to talk to her before he was detained by the police.

Professionally, she was thrilled at the pictures and interviews, but at times she had to dash tears from her eyes in order to see through her camera viewfinder. Some photojournalists could be hard-boiled and objective in the face of tragedy, but she had never developed that protective shell.

She caught glimpses of Mack helping with the rescue. His tall physique and broad shoulders stood out. The sight brought a hurting lump to her throat. She looked away, trying not to think about their personal lives.

By noon, all of the plane's passengers had been airlifted to hospitals or hotels in Monterrey.

Dusty was waiting to catch a ride on the last helicopter when Mack approached her. "The federal police are very interested in what I told them about José Guzmán and his ranch. They're sending a couple of police helicopters down there to take a look. Want to come along?"

"You bet!" Dusty exclaimed, quickly loading a fresh roll of film in her camera.

Again, Mack acted as a guide. With them in the helicopter were two heavily armed men in uniform. Another helicopter followed them.

When they spotted the ranch, the pilot circled the area at a low level.

"It looks deserted," one of the men in an officer's uniform said in Spanish.

"I'm not surprised," Mack answered. "When we escaped, they knew it wouldn't be long before we had the police down on their necks. They probably scattered."

"We'll find them," the officer muttered.

They landed and searched the grounds. As Mack suspected, they found a large marijuana field. "They're a bad bunch," the officer said. "We've had reports of bandits operating out of this area, preying on tourists, trafficking drugs. They won't get away from us."

Then the officer bowed politely to Dusty. "The *señora* would like a hotel room after such an adventure?" he asked gallantly in English. "We have very fine hotels in Monterrey. I tell the pilot to fly you there."

"Oh, *gracias, señor,*" Dusty replied with heartfelt gratitude. "Right now I'd trade my most expensive camera for a good meal, a warm bath and a soft bed."

The officer snapped an order to the helicopter pilot. In no time they were in the air again. Before dark they landed at a police heliport in Monterrey. From there, they took a taxi to one of the city's leading hotels.

The hotel was swarming with media people. Dusty spotted people she knew from the AP, the major TV networks, *Time*, *Newsweek*, *Life*, as well as many overseas correspondents. The hijacking had been the top news story for over forty-eight hours as the world waited tensely to learn the fate of the airliner. Now the correspondents were scrambling to get photographs and human-interest stories of the rescue.

Dusty thought about the priceless rolls of film in her camera bag and grinned smugly. The best these people could do would be photos of the hijack victims being brought to Monterrey by helicopter and perhaps some interviews now that the hijacking was over. But she had the real eyewitness story from the moment the drama had begun, from the hijackers' first shouts right up to the airlift. And she could back up the story with dozens of dramatic photographs.

She was the gal with the big scoop. By tomorrow this time, Dusty Landers was going to be the hottest name in photojournalism! The thought sent her blood racing.

When they walked through the plush lobby of the luxurious hotel, Dusty sighed. "Oh, this looks like heaven!" Looking at Mack, she said, "No offense, but your cave left something to be desired."

"I didn't hear any complaints at the time."

Dusty blushed furiously. As they approached the desk, she stopped him with a hand on his arm. "I want a separate room."

He looked surprised. "Why?"

"Mack, I am not sleeping with you again until we get our personal life straightened out."

He scowled. "Dusty, don't be so stubborn. The cave may not have been a luxury hotel, but the love we shared there must have convinced you that we belong together."

Tears stung her eyes. "That didn't prove a thing except that we're great in bed together and I already knew that. Now, either get me a separate bedroom or I'm going to another hotel."

He sighed. "Well, all right. I'll see if we can get adjoining suites."

"Just so there's a door between them that I can lock."

He raised an eyebrow. "You don't trust me?"

"About as much as I'd trust a pet rabbit with a boa constrictor."

"Thanks for the vote of confidence."

While Mack was busy registering at the desk, Dusty went to a phone booth. She made two calls. One was to the airport, where she booked the earliest flight she could get that would take her to New York, the other to her agent. She had some problems dealing with the Mexican telephone system, but the long-distance connection finally went through.

When Myra heard Dusty's voice she burst into tears. "Dusty! Oh, thank God you're alive. I've been out of my mind with worry. Are you all right?"

"I'm in Monterrey. I'm fine, Myra. Tired and dirty, but I'm all in one piece."

"Are you sure? We've been hearing all kinds of ghastly rumors—that the hijackers shot several people, that half the passengers died in the crash...."

"Yeah, well, you're going to get the real story from me," Dusty said, her voice tense with excitement.

"That's what I'm calling about. Myra, I've got the biggest scoop of my career! I was an eyewitness to the whole thing from the moment the hijackers pulled their guns. I was with the first helicopters that reached the crash site this morning. I talked with the passengers, the flight crew..."

Suddenly, her voice was choked in a flood of emotion. She had tried not to brood about the human suffering, but now the feelings engulfed her again—the fright, the heart-wrenching pity, the anger. For a moment she was overwhelmed.

With a determined effort, she regained control of her feelings. "Myra, I even had a chance to talk with the hijackers before they were taken into custody. One of them was willing to tell me everything, who they are, why they hijacked the plane, how they smuggled the guns on board. They're revolutionaries who have friends in a Central American prison. They planned to have the pilot land the plane in Central America and hold the crew and passengers hostage until their revolutionary friends were freed from prison. I got the whole interview on tape. And here's the best part, Myra, I have pictures. Great pictures. Shots of the whole thing from the moment the hijackers took over to the rescue this morning. I can show the whole world what happened—what those poor people went through."

Myra laughed almost hysterically. "Dusty, it's so good to hear you rattling on like that without taking a breath. Now I know you're all right. How soon can you get the pictures and tapes to me?"

"I'm bringing them myself. I'm not about to trust something like this to a delivery service. The earliest flight I can get out of here leaves at midnight. That'll give me a few hours to clean up and get a little rest before I grab a taxi for the airport. I have to change planes once, but I'll be in New York by early tomorrow morning. I'll get my film to the lab the minute I'm in Manhattan and get them to rush the processing through immediately. I'll have contact prints and the tape recordings on your desk before lunch."

"Terrific. I'll set up appointments with *Time*, *Newsweek*, some of the networks..."

"That sounds good."

"Dusty, I'm delighted about the story, but the best news is that you're okay."

"Well, I'll see you in the morning. Oh...Myra."

"Yes?"

"The Hollywood interview with Grant Packer that I was on my way to do when we got hijacked. Is it still on?"

"Oh, sure. After all this, you'll be something of a celebrity and heroine yourself. Grant ought to be even happier to talk to you. Want me to call him?"

"Yes, please. I'll need a day or two in New York to wind up this story and get a little rest, then I'll go on to Hollywood."

"Fine. I'll talk to Grant's publicity people and set up the interview for later this week." She hesitated, then asked, "Dusty...I don't mean to pry, but you know how I worry about you. How are things with you and Mack?"

"I'm—I'm not sure at the moment. He was on the flight with me."

Myra was momentarily speechless. "He was?"

"As a matter of fact, Mack turned out to be quite a hero. It was Mack who overpowered the gunman and then hiked down the mountain and brought help. I was with him. On the way we got captured by bandits . . . well, it's a long story."

"Good heavens! Then things are patched up between the two of you?"

"I don't know. We really haven't had time to talk about our personal life much. Mack's the cause of all our problems. If he'd give up this ridiculous, stubborn notion of forcing me to give up my career, everything would be fine. I'm going to try and talk some sense into him tonight. But you know how muleheaded Mack can be once he makes up his mind about something. He's practically issued me an ultimatum—become a full-time wife or else. Unless he backs down, I'm afraid it's going to mean the end of our marriage."

"Oh, Dusty, I hope you can work something out with him—some kind of compromise. I know you love Mack. Is a career worth your marriage?"

"Now don't you start in on me, Myra! You're supposed to be on my side. You know how much my career means to me. I'd dry up and die inside if I had to throw away everything I've worked for. I'd wind up hating Mack for dictating my life and I'd hate myself for giving in. Either way, our marriage would go on the rocks. It's one of those no-win situations, Myra. Look, I've got to go now. I want to soak in a tub and then get something to eat. I'm starved. I'll see you in the morning."

She hung up and stepped out of the phone booth.

Mack was waiting in the lobby. "What took you so long?"

"I was on the phone to Myra. Did you get the rooms?"

"I was able to get two suites connected by a door that you can lock." He handed her a key. "Does that make you happy?"

"Yes." She would die before admitting it to Mack, but in her heart she was thinking that the lock was a protection against her weakness for him.

Then she said, "Before I can go up to the room I have to do some shopping. There's no telling when they'll bring our luggage down from the crash site. All I have are the clothes on my back."

"Yeah, I'm in the same fix," Mack said. "There are some shops across the street."

"Let's go see what we can find."

They crossed the street and entered a clothing store. Mack pointed out a colorful Mexican dress and blouse. "You'd look good in that."

Dusty grinned. "A bit of a change from my usual jeans."

"Well, you may have to change your style. They don't carry American jeans here."

"How about this for you?" Dusty picked up a large sombrero from a counter and plopped it on Mack's head, then draped a serape over his shoulder. Mack struck a pose as Dusty stepped back to survey the effect.

"Terrific. You look like one of José Guzmán's gang. Don't know how you'd explain the red hair, though."

"Let's see how you look in the dress."

The clerk, who spoke English about as well as Dusty spoke Spanish, led her to a dressing room. The Mexican garment was a frilly gathered skirt with ruffles and intricate embroidery in gay, bright colors. With it was a white peasant blouse with puffed sleeves that could be pulled down to bare the shoulders.

Dusty felt self-conscious; the dress was totally out of character.

She stepped out of the dressing room. At Mack's long, intense look, she blushed, feeling oddly shy.

"Turn around," Mack said softly.

She looked at Mack again. His eyes were warm with approval.

"You're absolutely lovely, Dusty. You . . . you look so feminine. It's perfect for your coloring."

"Just the thing for a little Indian girl?"

"Right!"

"Well, it's completely impractical. But I don't have any other choice if I want to change into something clean." She returned to the dressing room to get back into her jeans and shirt. She would wait until she had a chance to clean up before changing clothes.

After emerging from the dressing room for the second time, she asked the clerk for lingerie in her size, then had it wrapped with the skirt and blouse.

Meanwhile, Mack had been in another dressing room. He appeared attired in trousers and shirt that had pearl buttons and fancy stitching around the pockets and seams. Around his waist was a wide, tooled belt with a large silver buckle.

"Looks like you're ready to go to a bullfight," Dusty observed.

Mack surveyed his reflection in a mirror. "I like it. Gives me a macho image."

It sure does, Dusty thought, with an unwanted quickening of her pulse. The tight pants revealed the muscular strength of his thighs and hugged the contours of his buttocks. The shirt made his strong shoulders seem even broader.

Looking at him, she felt a stirring of desire that spread through her like a warm flush. With a great effort, she wrenched her gaze from him. This was dangerous, she thought, forcibly reminding herself that she was trying to keep a level head around Mack until they sorted out their problems. This was no time to let her emotions rule her better judgment.

Mack also changed back into his other clothes. They left the shop carrying their packages. In the hotel, Dusty stopped at the desk and had her priceless rolls of exposed film put in the hotel safe. She couldn't afford to take chances.

Then they took the elevator. Mack paused, gave her a peculiar look, then went to the next door down the hall that was the entrance to his suite. Dusty felt depressed. This was all wrong. A part of her yearned for them to be sharing the same room, the same bed. With a sigh, she unlocked her door and entered her suite.

It was plush, with deep carpets and elegant, hand-crafted mahogany furniture.

The first thing she did was lock the door that connected her suite with Mack's. She had a peculiar feeling, knowing he was on the other side of the door, a feeling she couldn't exactly define. It seemed unnatural for them to be separated like this. She was suddenly lonely, longing to be with him. They'd been so close, had shared so much the past three days—terror, adventure, joy, despair, brushes with death and the exhilaration of success. Now this locked door had shut him out of her life.

Chapter Seven

Dusty made an effort to regain a firm grip on her resolve. She was determined not to give in at this point, not until he came to his senses. He had wounded her deeply when he had moved out of their apartment without a word. It had been a form of desertion, in spite of what he said. He had caught up with her in Dallas, apparently in an effort to patch things up. But nothing he had said so far had convinced her he was changing his attitude about her career.

She discarded her grimy jeans and shirt, leaving a trail of clothes all the way to the bathroom. She was filled with the anticipation of a long, soaking bath, the first she'd had in three days.

The bathroom was anything but disappointing. Spacious, with white and gold tiles, a vanity countertop and thick, white rugs on the floor, it exuded luxury. But it was the elegant, large sunken tub that beckoned to her. She turned the gold-plated faucet handles and poured a generous quantity of bubble bath and scented bath oil. She uttered a soft moan of delight as she sank into a warm ocean of fragrant soapy bubbles.

She closed her eyes in ecstasy as the warm water caressed her tired body and comforted her aching muscles. She squirmed in the thick blanket of bubbles, wiggling her toes, running her hands over her shoulders and arms, lifting a knee and watching the soapy water trickle down a gleaming thigh before she plunged it back under the surface. She flicked the suds with a thumb and forefinger and giggled like a child with her rubber duck.

"A lovely sight," drawled a masculine voice.

Dusty gasped, her startled gaze turning toward the doorway. There stood Mack, casually leaning against the doorjamb, arms folded, a teasing smile on his lips as his eyes drank in the sight.

"How did you get in my suite?" Dusty demanded furiously. "I locked the door."

He dangled a key. "I unlocked it."

Her eyes narrowed. "How did you get that key?"

"Bribed the maid."

"Get out of here."

"Why? I'm enjoying the view."

She glared at him, then grabbed a bar of soap and flung it as hard as she could.

He ducked, laughing. "Keep that up and I'll withdraw my offer of dinner."

"What offer?"

"I thought after all the excitement of the past few days you'd enjoy a leisurely meal in your room, so I took the liberty of phoning room service. How does oysters Rockefeller, quail, wild rice, vegetables, a flaming dessert and a bottle of champagne strike you?"

Her mouth watered. "It sounds heavenly, but what happened to your usual wheat germ, yogurt, raw salad and vegetable juice?"

"Not on the menu. What the hell? Tonight calls for a celebration. How about it? Have dinner with me, Mrs. O'Shea?"

"I'll consider it if you'll get out and let me finish my bath."

"I'm not in any rush. As I said, I'm enjoying the view."

She tried to ignore the nervous tingle caused by the look in Mack's hungry eyes. Grinning wickedly, she raised one gleaming knee above the water's edge. Mack's gaze became more intense. He moved away from the doorjamb, toward the tub.

She waited until he was within a few feet of the sunken tub. Then her hand came out of the water, holding a dripping facecloth. She threw it with deadly accuracy right in his face.

Dusty howled with laughter as Mack spluttered and groped for a towel to wash the soap out of his eyes.

"You little—"

"Mack, no!" she screamed.

But he moved quickly and knelt beside the tub before he gave her head a firm push, ducking her.

This time it was she who was spluttering as she came out of the water. "My eyes!" she gasped.

Mack handed her a towel. Once the soap was out of her eyes, she grabbed two fistfuls of his shirt and pulled with all her might.

Mack gave a startled cry. For a second he teetered on the edge of the tub, caught off balance, then went in with a splash. Waves of bubble bath sloshed out onto the floor. Mack floundered in the water, grabbed Dusty and gave her another ducking. She was laughing so hard she swallowed a generous amount of soapy water. When she caught her breath, she stared at Mack sitting beside her in the tub fully clothed, and started laughing all over again.

Mack looked ruefully down at his soggy clothes, stuck to his arms and legs. His hair was pasted to his forehead in dripping strands. He glared at Dusty. She was sitting up, rivulets of soapy water trickling between her exposed breasts, which quivered as she laughed. The wicked grin returned to Mack's lips and his hands found her body under the water.

"Now, wait a minute." She pushed him away. "I told you I wasn't sleeping with you again until we got our personal problems straightened out."

"Why don't we make love and then talk about it?"

"I've got a better idea. Why don't you go back to your room, get out of those wet clothes and let me finish my bath. Then we'll have a nice, relaxed dinner."

"And after dinner . . . then maybe you'll be in a romantic mood?"

"I'm not promising anything. Go take a cold shower." She splashed water at him.

Mack looked frustrated but gave in. "I guess I don't cut a very romantic figure in these wet clothes. Good thing I hadn't changed into the new outfit I bought."

"You look like a half-drowned rat," she teased. "And I do mean rat. Of all the underhanded, low-down tricks . . . bribing the maid!"

He shrugged. "All's fair in love and war."

She looked at him for a moment, growing quiet. What was it going to be? she wondered. Love or war?

Mack got out of the tub, muttering as he squeezed the surplus water out of his clothing. When he was able to leave the bathroom without dripping a trail of soapy water with every step, he returned to his suite.

Dusty drained the tub, then rinsed bubble bath from her body with a stream of clear water. She stepped out of the tub and dried off with a thick bath towel, rubbing herself until her skin glowed. After drying with the towel, she used it to mop up the water that had splashed on the floor when she pulled Mack into the tub. She dried her hair and brushed it until it shone with highlights.

Then she slipped into the fresh new lingerie and the Mexican skirt and blouse. She gazed at the transformation reflected in the mirror. In the shop she had joked about the dress being right for a little Indian girl. But certain clothes did bring out her heritage. This skirt and blouse emphasized the dusky rose hue of her complexion and the startling darkness of her eyes.

She pulled the blouse down, baring her throat and shoulders. The outfit gave her an acute sense of her femininity. She had a wave of anxiety, wishing her jeans weren't too soiled to wear. In this costume, she felt strangely vulnerable.

Before the evening ended, was she going to forget her resolve to keep out of Mack's bed? After all, would that be such a mistake? Perhaps if they shared a romantic dinner followed by a passionate interlude, Mack might come to his senses and realize what he was throwing away. It was a dangerously tempting thought.

Dusty visualized the evening before them, the tender words, the fiery passion and then Mack admitting he was wrong to try to dictate her life, to make her over into someone else. Everything would be back like it was before.

She took her time getting ready. The natural, soft blush of her complexion inherited from her Indian grandmother made it unnecessary to apply artificial coloring. Her high cheekbones created soft shadows in the contours of her cheeks. The overall effect of the raven-black hair, winged eyebrows, jet-black eyes, high cheekbones and generous mouth gave a hint of untamed wildness, like a bird born to fly high and free in the vast blue sky.

There was a tap at the bathroom door. "Dinner has been served," Mack announced.

"Since when did you bother to knock?"

"I don't want to get dunked in the bathtub again." Dusty grinned.

Mack had made an attempt to comb his unruly dark red hair into some semblance of order. He had changed into the shirt and trousers he had bought in the Mexican shop. Dusty thought, her pulse quickening, that it wasn't fair for one man to be so attractive.

His rugged features might not win any beauty contests, but he sure had more than his share of sex appeal.

The expression in his eyes when he surveyed the effect of her colorful skirt and blouse made her weak-kneed.

Room service had set up the table with a linen tablecloth, candles and a centerpiece of fresh roses. Beside the table in a bucket of ice was the champagne.

"Does this hotel usually do things with such style?" Dusty asked.

"They do if you tip them enough."

"Boy, they're going to love you around here—first the maid, then room service."

"Well, this is a special occasion," he said, pulling a chair out for her. He plucked one of the roses from the centerpiece, tucked the blossom into her hair and stepped back to survey the effect. "Just the added touch that costume needed. Now you really look the part of a *señorita* with fiery Indian blood in her veins."

"What's this special occasion you're talking about?" she asked.

"Us getting back together."

He worked the champagne cork loose with a flourish and it popped loudly. He filled two glasses with the foaming liquid and took a seat across the table from her. "To us, Dusty," he said, raising his glass.

She hesitated. "Are we—back together, Mack?"

"Sure. No more problems, right?"

She wasn't sure of his meaning, but let his comment pass for the moment. She didn't think the tim-

ing was quite right for the showdown they were certain
to have before the evening ended.

Mack's gaze lingered on her face. "Dusty, you're
absolutely beautiful in the candlelight."

She felt a throbbing tingle all through her body at
the adoring way Mack was looking at her.

She kept the conversation light during the meal. As
usual, she did most of the talking. "I keep thinking
about the expression on José Guzmán's face when I
took his picture. There he was, all tied up, with his
pants down around his ankles. Boy, that must have
been a blow to his macho image. I can't wait to get
that picture developed. I'm going to have an enlarge-
ment made and hang it on my apartment wall."

She suddenly felt a wave of sadness as she thought
how, without thinking, she had said, "my apartment
wall." It should have been "our apartment wall." But
Mack had moved out. It was no longer "our" apartment. She wondered if it was going to be "our"
apartment again after tonight. Was that what Mack
had meant when he'd said, "No more problems"?

She touched the rose Mack had placed over her ear
and felt as vulnerable as the delicate flower. Mack ate
slowly, leaning back to stare silently at her from time
to time as she rattled on.

At one point he placed his hands over hers, making
her voice catch. She tried to keep her treacherous
breath even as she stared at his long, tapered fingers.
The dark hairs curling there reminded her of the hair
on his chest, on his body, on his legs.

She looked at him, startled at her own reaction.
How could this man unleash such a torrent of desire
in her? She chewed her bottom lip for a minute and

tried to decide whether to indulge herself by leaving her hand in Mack's. He smiled. She squeezed his hand. An electric jolt ran through her. He gave her hand a knowing squeeze in return and winked.

She retrieved her hand and stared at it thoughtfully. Was she doing the right thing?

"Mack . . ." she began.

"Shh," he said softly, placing a raised finger to her lips. "You talk too much."

Her lips burned where their skin had made contact. She ached for him to hold her, to kiss her. His finger on her mouth was but a hint of what was to come. She closed her eyes and sat back in her chair, remembering other times, other places, other nights. . . .

They finished the meal. Dusty was feeling a pleasant, relaxed glow from the good food and the champagne.

The music from the hotel's sound system had provided a soft, melodic background. Now those same sounds seemed to pulsate through her. She was disturbingly aware of Mack, of the texture of his rugged skin, of the sheen of his dark red hair, of the rustle of his trousers as he rose. He moved to her side of the table and took her hands again. His fingers felt warm and strong. He was gazing directly into her eyes. She felt her breath quicken, her heartbeat accelerate.

He drew her to her feet. Dusty thought she would drown in the depth of his gaze. She was falling under a kind of spell that shut out everything except this intense moment they were sharing. Then his lips were on hers, touching off a chain reaction of electric sensations.

Was she making a mistake? If they made love, would anything change? It might only make her heartbreak worse.

But maybe it would make a difference to him. Maybe Mack would come to his senses and see that his need for her was greater than their differences.

Or was she overestimating his need for her? It was a chance she would have to take.

Her arms crept around his neck. For this magic moment, everything was blotted from her mind except the passion that had inflamed her.

"Mack..." she said weakly, "I—I'm not sure this is a very good idea...."

"Why not?"

"I've already told you...it doesn't solve anything...."

Instead of replying, he kissed her again. She felt dizzy. His mouth captured hers and held it for a long, tantalizing minute. Then he parted her lips with his tongue and explored the velvet softness in the hidden depths. Involuntarily, she dug her fingernails into the nape of his neck, her body tensing with rising passion.

He pulled her into the curve of his body, crushing her to his masculine shape. She melted willingly against him, her senses reeling.

His trembling fingers pushed her peasant blouse all the way down from her shoulders. He buried his face in the exposed cleavage of her breasts. She sucked her breath in sharply at the caress of his lips.

"I want you, Dusty," he said, his voice husky. "I want you now...." He reached behind her and unhooked her strapless bra. It fell away, exposing her firm mounds to the cool air.

Mack looked at her, his eyes taking in the sight of her exposed twin peaks. He smiled. "And you want me, too," he said.

So her body had given her away. As if he didn't know already!

She drew a shaky breath, conscious of her throbbing pulse.

He drew her closer, looking deep into her eyes, waiting for the sign of consent she knew he could read there.

She was angry with herself for the chance she was taking with her feelings, but it was too late now. The mounting tide of passion controlled the situation.

His lips crushed down on hers and all rational thought was scattered to the four winds. She moaned softly. His hands slipped down her back, cupping her hips, pulling her up against him.

She thought, *Oh, it's just one night....*

Mack swept her up in his arms and carried her to the bed. He placed her gently on the velvet bedspread and kissed her again, his breathing deep and raspy. The sound created an explosion of fire in her. She pulled his head down to her breasts, willingly offering herself for their mutual satisfaction.

Then he slipped her arms from the blouse and pulled it down over her skirt. She unbuttoned his shirt, slowly stretching out the agonizing anticipation. She didn't want it to be over too soon.

As Mack shrugged out the sleeves, Dusty ran the tips of her fingers down the back of his arm. Goose bumps popped out and he moaned.

"I'll give you just five minutes to stop that," he teased, "before we go on to something more interesting."

When she saw the scar in his shoulder, she touched it gently. Then she trailed her fingers down his chest, lightly scratching all the way.

Mack picked up her hands and kissed her fingertips. Then he nibbled them lightly, gazing at her with a wicked gleam in his eyes. Slowly he moved her hands down to his belt buckle and placed them firmly against it. He looked at her questioningly.

She nodded and flipped the leather width loose. Then she reached for the zipper....

A few moments later Mack stepped out of his trousers. He stood there looking like an Olympic athlete.

Dusty swallowed hard, her nerves screaming with tension. Mack lifted one knee and rested it on the bed, making the mattress sag from his weight. Dusty rolled in his direction. As she did so, he tucked his thumbs in the waistband of her skirt and gently pulled downward. Dusty reached for the button and unfastened it. The skirt slipped down easily. Mack held it up with one thumb and then rakishly tossed it over his shoulder.

"Come here, *señora*," he said huskily as he pulled her to him and rained kisses over her neck and throat.

The rose Mack had placed over her ear fell to the bed. Dusty was only vaguely aware that she had lost it. Was she losing something else?

Urgent, pressing desires held her captive. This was Mack. She was Dusty. They were two people made for each other. When they made love, there were no barriers between them. It was the one time that their marriage was heavenly. In bed they had no arguments.

Even if she had wanted to, she couldn't turn back now, not with Mack making love to her, propelling her to the heights of ecstasy as only he could do. He knew every place that inflamed her passion, and he touched them all. She moaned with hunger for him as he sought to satisfy her longing.

She was consumed with a burning desire. It grew and grew as Mack took her to greater and greater heights of pleasure and intimacy. And then the flames became a raging inferno that died into smoldering embers, flared anew and finally subsided into a warm afterglow.

Resting close to him, curled against his body, Dusty sighed contentedly. It was a beautiful moment. Dreamily, she listened to Mack's voice, to the soothing masculine timbre and quality rather than the words. Only gradually did she become conscious of what he was actually saying.

She frowned. "What was that you said?"

"I was talking about Dallas. You're going to like it there, Dusty. I thought we might get an apartment for a while and then start looking for a house. No need to be in a rush about buying a place, but eventually that's what we're going to do. I've had my fill of rooms and apartments. A place of our own somewhere in the suburbs would be great. Two stories. I always liked two-story homes. We had a big, roomy two-story house where I grew up in Louisiana...."

She sat up, her eyes blazing. "Wait a minute, Mack O'Shea. How did we suddenly wind up in a two-story home in Dallas?"

"What's wrong with a two-story home? You've got something against stairs?"

"I've got something against the direction this conversation is taking. What's wrong with keeping the apartment in New York?"

"There's no point in it. My job is in Dallas. You won't be chasing all over the world anymore. There'll be no need for you to hang around New York."

Dusty's narrowed eyes turned into hot black coals. "So we're back to the same old argument. You haven't changed one bit, have you, Mack O'Shea? I thought after what we've been through together the past three days, that night in the cave, almost getting shot by José Guzmán and his band of cutthroats, making love tonight...you'd come to your senses and realize what we have between us is what is important—not where we live or where my career takes me...."

Mack frowned. "And I thought nearly getting killed in that crash landing would bring you to your senses, Dusty. What kind of life is it, not knowing if you're going to wake up dead or alive?"

"That hasn't got anything to do with my career."

"Of course it does. Do you know how many correspondents and photojournalists were killed or kidnapped last year?"

"Well, sure there's some risk, but—"

"There's more than a risk. You take too many chances, more than most reporters. I think you like the thrill of seeing how close you can get to the edge."

"No, I don't. I like my job and I want to be the best in my business. Maybe that involves taking some chances, but I know what I'm doing."

"Well, I don't like it."

Tears of anger blurred Dusty's vision. "So you're going to make my life over."

"No, Dusty," Mack said, in his plodding, patient manner, which somehow right now only made her madder. "You know how I feel about this situation. We can't have a marriage with you chasing all over the globe and me not knowing if my wife is alive or dead in an airplane crash or a shoot-out between fanatics in some alley, God knows where."

"You knew about my career when you married me. Remember, I knew you were a CIA agent. CIA agents get bumped off all the time. I worried about you a lot, but I just accepted that worrying came with the territory. I said a prayer for you every night. That didn't change how I felt about you and I didn't try to get you to quit."

Mack sighed. "That was all right for a while. Then I started getting fed up with the whole scene. I thought you'd grow up and get tired of playing games, too."

"Games?" she repeated furiously. "Do you call what I'm doing a game?"

"Yeah, now that you mention it. I think it's a way you have of ducking the responsibility of a marriage, a home, raising a family...."

"That's a cheap shot, Mack O'Shea. I want to start a family in a few years. There'll come a time when I'm ready. But first I have things to do, places to see."

He gave her a searching look. "What are you trying to prove, anyway, Dusty? Was it growing up with two brothers? You have to prove you can do what the big boys do? Does it have something to do with that dreary little crossroads store and gas station where you grew up and the Indian reservation where your grandmother lived? Do you have to make it big to show the world and mainly yourself that you pulled yourself up by your bootstraps and became a big success?''

"Oh, now I'm getting the psychoanalysis bit. Do you charge by the hour, Dr. O'Shea? If we're going to start psychoanalyzing each other, maybe we could delve into your psyche, and find out what gives you the macho, male-chauvinist idea that I'm a child and you have to dictate what I should eat, what time I should go to bed and how I should change my life-style and career to suit your plans!''

"So we're getting down to name-calling, are we?''

"You started it. You said I was an irresponsible child who was ducking the responsibility of marriage.''

"No, I didn't.''

"Maybe not in so many words, but that's what you meant.''

"Well, that's what it looks like from where I stand. I'm not asking you to turn into a housewife. You could get into some work in Dallas—maybe local TV reporting or newspaper journalism....''

Dusty's breathing was labored, her eyes narrowed and glaring. It was hard for her to believe she had loved Mack O'Shea with such abandon less than a half hour before. Now they were suddenly strangers.

"Do you know what I think? I think you made a mistake when you married me instead of Laura Nicholson. She'd be exactly the kind of settled, predictable homemaker and mother that you want for a wife.''

"I don't know about that, but at least I can have a discussion with Laura without the danger of getting scalped. There's just no point in talking to a Cherokee when she's on the warpath."

"Not any more than trying to reason with a stubborn, bullheaded Irishman named Mack O'Shea!"

With that parting shot, Dusty lay back down and stared at the ceiling, her fists clutched at her sides.

A cold, distant silence settled over them. Mack sighed and turned on his side, his back to her.

The minutes dragged by. After a while, Dusty heard Mack's steady breathing; he had fallen asleep.

She slipped out of bed and checked her wristwatch. It was time to go to the airport and catch her plane for New York. She dressed in her new clothes, went to her suite, picked up her trench coat and slung her camera bag over her shoulder.

She walked softly back into Mack's bedroom. For a moment, she stood by his side, looking down at his sleeping figure. Then she slipped off her wedding ring, and pinned it to the pillow beside him.

For a moment, she looked at the bed, tears blurring her vision. Then she walked out of the room and out of Mack O'Shea's life.

IT'S A JACKPOT OF A GREAT OFFER!

- 4 exciting Silhouette Special Edition novels—FREE!
- a folding umbrella—FREE!
- a surprise mystery bonus that will delight you—FREE!

Silhouette Folding Umbrella— ABSOLUTELY FREE

You'll love your Silhouette umbrella. Its bright color will cheer you up on even the gloomiest day. It's made of rugged nylon to last for years, and is so compact (folds to 15") you can carry it in your purse or briefcase. This folding umbrella is yours free with this offer.

But wait . . . there's even more!

Money-Saving Home Delivery!

Subscribe to Silhouette Special Edition and enjoy the convenience of previewing new, hot-off-the-press books every month, delivered right to your home. Each book is yours for only $1.95—55¢ less per book than what you pay in stores! And there's no extra charge for postage and handling.

Special Extras—Free!

You'll also get our free monthly newsletter—the indispensable insider's look at our most popular writers and their upcoming novels. Now you can have a behind-the-scenes look at the fascinating world of Silhouette. It's an added bonus you'll look forward to every month. You'll also get additional free gifts from time to time as a token of our appreciation for being a home subscriber.

Mail this card today for
4 FREE BOOKS
this folding umbrella and
a mystery gift ALL FREE!

Chapter Eight

It was a weary, saddened Dusty O'Shea who boarded the plane for New York. She sat huddled, staring blankly out of the window like a lost, lonely child. Inside, she felt a vast emptiness. As the plane took off, she was aware of a dreadful sense of loss, as if she were leaving behind a vital part of her being. She couldn't swallow the aching lump that filled her throat. The months she had shared with Mack since their marriage were reduced to a montage of bittersweet memories.

Finally, worn out by the battle between grief and anger, she fell into an exhausted sleep.

"Not bad for a morning's work," Myra said the following day over lunch. "In addition to AP grabbing the story, *Newsweek* wants an expanded feature article. Also you're scheduled for interviews on *World News Tonight* and *Good Morning America* with some of the pictures and taped interviews. This could earn you an award.''

''I'm absolutely bushed,'' Dusty said wearily. ''In the past forty-eight hours, the only sleep I've had was on the flight from Mexico. The night before that I spent bouncing down a primitive mountain road in a Jeep and the night before that, half-frozen in a mountain cave, wondering if a bear or mountain lion was going to wander in any minute, looking for an evening meal. Then I haven't stopped running since I got off the plane this morning.''

''I know you're exhausted,'' Myra sympathized. ''But you have to be in the studio soon to tape that evening news segment. Then you can get some rest.''

''Until 5:00 a.m. when the alarm goes off so I can do *Good Morning America*. But I guess I shouldn't complain. This is the big story of my career.''

''You'd better believe it. Every other journalist in the country is turning green.''

Dusty was savoring this moment of relaxation, sipping a wine spritzer as they waited for lunch to be served. They had stopped at one of Myra's favorite haunts, a small French restaurant on East Forty-third street.

As hectic as the pace had been, Dusty welcomed the pressure. It kept her from thinking about Mack and the agony of finally having to accept that their marriage was hopeless. In this momentary lull, it again caught up with her. She felt a wave of depression. A sudden stinging in her eyes warned that tears were very near the surface.

Myra, in addition to being her agent, was her closest friend, a friendship that went back several years. She gazed at Dusty thoughtfully. "Things aren't working out so well between you and Mack, are they?" she asked sympathetically.

Dusty gave her a startled look. "Myra, sometimes the way you read my thoughts is downright eerie."

"It doesn't exactly take a soothsayer to see you're miserable."

"That obvious, huh?"

"Any time Dusty O'Shea is quiet, I know something is seriously wrong." Myra gave her hand a comforting squeeze.

"Well, don't go getting sympathetic on me. I'm on the verge of bawling now."

"I feel for you, Dusty. I know having a marriage come unglued is devastating. It happened to me, you know."

"Yes, I know, Myra. How long did it take you to get over Jim?"

"Well, I don't know yet. It's only been three years."

"Well, that's damn encouraging!"

"It does get so you can live with it after the first awful months." Myra took a sip of her spritzer. "Wasn't there any kind of compromise you and Mack could work out?"

"There's no compromising with that man. He's got his stubborn Irish head made up. The only way we could patch things up is for me to give up my career and submit to him for the rest of my life."

Myra twisted the stem of her glass thoughtfully. "Perhaps Mack isn't the only one who's being stubborn," she suggested tentatively.

Dusty sighed. "Yeah, you're right, of course. I've got my heels dug in, too. Believe me, Myra, I've lost a lot of sleep wrestling with myself, wondering if I could make myself over to suit him." She shook her head. "It simply wouldn't work. I'd wind up hating myself—hating him. At this point in my life, I'm just not ready for what Mack wants. My career means too much. It's terrible, trying to decide between a career and the man you love. But it's more than just the career. I'd have to smother my own individuality, change myself into something I'm not. I'd spend every day living a lie. If Mack would just give me more time! Maybe in a few years I'd be ready for what he wants. But he wants it now. He's older, more settled. That's what I get for falling for an older man. At the time we met, I didn't think it would be a problem. He was with the CIA. We didn't like being apart so much, but we accepted each other's careers and life-styles. Then Mack changed, but I didn't...."

"Maybe he'll change his mind now that you're separated."

"It's hopeless, Myra," Dusty argued. "But I can see his side of the matter. He's not being entirely unreasonable. Who wants to be married to a globe-trotting junkie like me? The poor guy is tired of living out of suitcases and wondering if his wife is going to get her stupid head blown off at any time. What it boils down to is that we're just incompatible. Mack deserves a wife who is ready to settle down and establish a home for him. I hate to say it, but I think he made a mistake when he broke off his engagement to Laura Nicholson. They'd known each other since college. She's the kind of woman who would give him a good, solid home. I think Mack regrets not marrying her, too, but he won't admit it."

"Maybe it was because Mack loves you."

"It isn't enough. We're at each other's throats all the time. What I want to do now is get on with my life. Which reminds me—how about that Hollywood interview with Grant Packer? Did you have time to do anything about that?"

"Yes, I did. I was on the phone to his secretary first thing this morning. It's all set for you to have the interview. But you're going to have to do some hopping around to keep up with him. You'll get a brief, preliminary interview at his home in Beverly Hills on Saturday. Then he's starting that new film on location, so you'll have to follow him if you want to see him in action. From what I've heard, trying to keep up with Grant Packer is like running a marathon."

"Don't worry about that," Dusty said confidently. "I can keep up with the best of them."

For the next three days, Dusty did not answer her telephone. She let her answering machine take all incoming calls. She thought that Mack would probably call her and she did not want to deal with talking to him.

By the time she left for California, there were a number of messages from Mack on her machine, beginning with: "Dusty, call me right away at the hotel in Monterrey."

The next recorded message on the machine said, "Dusty, I'm back in Dallas. Call me immediately. Here is my number..."

Then, "Dusty, damn it, I called Myra. I know you're in New York. I know you're getting my messages. Answer the damn telephone."

The next recorded message: "I called Myra again. She said you're going on to California after you finish your business in New York. Don't you do it, you hear me? We need to talk. If you won't come to Dallas, I'll fly to New York. Phone me."

The morning she left for California, she checked her machine. There was one final message from Mack. He sounded as if he had been drinking. "Go on to California. I don't give a damn. I hope you find Grant Packer as charming as all his other girlfriends do. I'm taking Laura Nicholson to dinner tonight."

Furious, Dusty picked up the answering machine. She was on the verge of hurling it across the room when she remembered how much it cost.

She almost called the airport and changed her flight reservation from Los Angeles to Dallas, then she regained her self-control. "Suit yourself, Mack O'Shea. I hope you and Laura Nicholson will be very happy!"

Tearfully, she picked up her suitcase and camera bag, stormed out of her apartment and caught a taxi for the airport.

Grant Packer. On the flight to Los Angeles, Dusty reviewed what she knew about the star, preparing for the in-depth personality piece she planned to write about him.

Since his Oscar-winning role in *Backlash*, Grant Packer had been the hottest name in the film industry. He was as well-known for his producing and directing as for his acting. The films that bore his name as producer-director all had the unmistakable Grant Packer touch—extravagant special effects, remarkable camera work, and most of all, unforgettable characters.

He was about to start production on a film that he'd also written, based on the life of Jack Dempsey, the famous heavyweight boxing champion of the 1920s. Packer, who had been a street fighter and amateur Golden Gloves boxer, was going to play the title role.

It would fit his Charles Bronson tough-guy image. Like Bronson, Packer was known for his roles as hard-bitten cops or streetwise fighters. In *Backlash*, he played the role of a tough ex-detective who had hit the skids but pulled himself out of the gutter to avenge the murder of a wife who had left him. He had taken the trite situation and had given it such an entirely new dimension that it had won him an academy award.

From what Dusty had read about Grant Packer, he was something of a dictator on film sets, demanding total commitment from the actors. He drove producers up the wall with his budget demands, spending whatever it took to get the desired effects. But he stuck to shooting schedules no matter how hard he had to drive actors and production crews. Those who worked with Grant Packer loved him, hated him or feared him. There was no middle ground in his relationships.

His personal life was flamboyant. Like his screen characters, he was larger than life. He gave extravagant parties. His personal friends ranged from sports figures to ex-presidents.

Articles published about him were not entirely flattering. While everyone agreed he was a man of towering talents, some writers described him as a despot who made unreasonable demands on actors and production staffs. It was said that his temper had a short fuse. His abusive comments to reporters were common knowledge.

He had been married twice. Recently his first wife had written a book about her life with him. It had been a hostile piece. Among other things, she described him as a self-centered egotist, too much in love with himself to care about anyone else.

When her plane landed in Los Angeles, Dusty phoned Grant Packer's secretary, who said they were expecting her. She took a taxi to Beverly Hills.

Packer lived in a mansion that had been built by a silent-movie star in the 1920s. Packer had renovated and modernized the spacious house and extensive grounds. Lush vegetation, including great palm trees and flowering bougainvillea, created a semitropical atmosphere. There was the usual Olympic-size swimming pool, a tennis court and a garage containing a half-dozen costly automobiles ranging from a Rolls-Royce to an all-terrain vehicle.

Dusty knew that Grant Packer had come from a very poor background. All this opulence, she deduced, could very well be a compensation for his earlier poverty.

She was greeted at the door by his secretary, who led Dusty through vast rooms to French doors that opened on the pool where Grant was sunning himself in a reclining deck lounge. Dusty had seen all his films and was well aware of how his masculine sex appeal radiated from the screen.

Meeting him was a physical experience. His movies had made his rough-tough countenance a familiar sight. His scarred face looked as if it had been redesigned by countless street fights. Yet it had a kind of crude handsomeness, as if it had been chiseled out of rough granite.

He uncoiled his six feet of brawn lazily from the lounge and smiled a warm greeting. He was dressed only in swimming trunks. He looked bronzed and fit; there wasn't an ounce of superfluous fat on his trim, hard waist.

"Mrs. O'Shea," he said in his familiar, gravelly voice with polite softness smoothing the rough edges. His large hand gripped her hand firmly. "It's a pleasure to meet you. I saw you on *Good Morning America* a couple of days ago. That was a pretty rough experience you went through."

"Yes, it was. I'm still having nightmares. I'm glad to be here and certainly pleased that you've agreed to this interview."

His unflinching gaze seemed to drill right into her. "I'm approached all the time by reporters and writers. I usually shy away from this kind of interview. But I've read some of your articles. I like your intelligent objectivity. And the publication that has you doing this piece has a halfway decent reputation, which is more than I can say for some of the trash on the newsstands. After the hatchet job my ex-wife did on me, I thought it might be a good idea if somebody who didn't have a personal ax to grind would publish the truth about me for a change. You might convince the public that I'm not the monster she makes me out to be. Hopefully, you can clear up some of the ridiculous lies floating around this town.''

After all the tough-guy roles, Dusty was surprised by his polished manner of speaking.

''I can promise I'll write only the truth—as I see it.''

His penetrating look was magnetic. He emanated a powerful, commanding presence. The strength of his personality was like a force field. She could easily see why he made such a strong director, why he was in command on the set. He was a born leader; he had charm and charisma, a gracious air of chivalry toward women and an underlying will of steel. One had to be careful around such personalities; it was easy to become hypnotized and fall under their spell.

Her first impression was that he did not seem to be the fire-breathing ogre his first wife had described or the hard-drinking nightclub brawler with a chip on his shoulder as some reporters had pictured him. True, his heavy dark brows, piercing green eyes and rough, scarred countenance would cause a person to think twice before crossing him. But under the tough exterior, there seemed to her to be an element of tenderness and politeness. Perhaps that explained his appeal to both male and female audiences. The men saw in his macho image a kind of beer-drinking, saloon-brawling buddy they could respect, while women sensed an innate gentleness and caring.

Still, she would reserve final judgment until she had the opportunity to know him better.

Now he relaxed and demonstrated his ability to be hospitable and charming. ''What can we do to make you comfortable? You must be thirsty and hungry after your flight.''

"Just a tall, cool soft drink, please." She smiled. "Have to keep my wits about me."

He gave the order to his secretary, who was hovering in the background. Then he gallantly adjusted one of the poolside lounge chairs for Dusty. She settled into it and Packer sat back on the one facing her.

He was a handsome rascal, all right, in his own way—like a diamond in the rough. She wondered about all the gossip about his romantic conquests.

He, also, was taking inventory of her features. The looks of interest in his eyes gave her a surge of adrenaline that any woman, if she were alive and breathing, couldn't help feeling.

There were certain things about Grant Packer that she did not have to ask—they were matters of record. His real name, she knew, was Jack Miller. His father was Caucasian, his mother Mexican. He had been born in a Texas border town. When he was three, his father deserted the family. His mother took Jack and the other children back to Mexico, where she had relatives.

He didn't have a trace of an accent. Speech coaches had taken care of that, of course, including any Texas drawl that might have been mixed in. There were traces of Hispanic ancestry in his luxurious, thick, wavy black hair, but he had his father's eyes that were an unusual deep green hue.

When he'd been a teenager, Jack Miller had returned to the States. He attended high school in Texas, then bummed around the country for several years, trying his hand at everything from oil-field work to singing in a country-and-western band. Ducking beer bottles and trading punches in those honky-tonks had probably earned him some of his scars.

He accidentally got a part in a film being made by a regional movie producer in Texas. Designed for the art-theater circuit, the film won the acclaim of critics. Something about Jack's earthy, masculine presence in the film, untrained though he was, caught the attention of a Hollywood producer. He signed Jack Miller to a contract, changed Jack's name to Grant Packer and arranged for some formal training. From that point, Jack—now Grant—had a career that took off like a skyrocket. He was a natural-born actor and he soaked up moviemaking techniques like a sponge. In no time he had starring roles, then moved on to directing and writing. Now, at thirty-five, he was at the peak of his popularity and success.

A servant brought Dusty's drink. She sipped it thirstily, welcoming the cool, sweet liquid.

"Well, when do we start?" Grant asked.

"We already have." She smiled.

He raised an eyebrow questioningly.

"I began taking notes from the first moment I saw you."

"Notes? I don't see any pad or tape recorder."

She laughed and tapped her temple. "Up here. I don't need a pad for this kind of article. And I don't give you the third degree. If this were a different kind of article—if you were a politician, for example—I'd be taking all kinds of notes. But the kind of personality story I want to do about you requires a different approach. What I'd like to do for a few days, if it's agreeable with you, is just hang around you when it fits your schedule, watch you working, chat with you now and then. You'll tell me all about yourself.''

"Oh, I will, will I?'' He scowled.

But he couldn't scare her with that tough-guy look. He might beat up guys in honky-tonks, but she was beginning to suspect that when it came to women, he was nothing but a big pussycat.

"Sure,'' she replied. "And a lot more honestly than if you carefully answered a list of stock questions.''

Packer's scowling countenance broke into a wide grin. He laughed. "Well, I think I'm going to like the part about you 'hanging around.' You're a very attractive young woman, Dusty O'Shea.''

She felt her cheeks warm. *Careful,* she thought. He'd been checking her out since she had stepped through the door and he liked what he saw. Somehow she was going to have to keep on good terms with him while she kept him at arm's distance, and she didn't think Grant Packer was used to that kind of treatment.

"There are a couple of things I'd like to ask you about,'' she said, steering the conversation away from anything personal. "This new film you're starting— the Jack Dempsey story. Why Jack Dempsey?''

His sea-green eyes became thoughtful. "Those times when Jack Dempsey fought, from around 1915 into the 1920s, fascinate me. It was an age of heroes—Charles Lindbergh, Babe Ruth, Gene Tunney. The setting—the speakeasies, hot jazz musicians, bathtub gin, flappers, cars like the Stutz Bearcats—all great material for mood and background. Dempsey himself was a product of hard times and rough little frontier towns. Men like Dempsey fought because they were hungry. They rode the rails, slept in hobo camps, fought in saloons for a few bucks.

"A biography about Dempsey described him as a 'hobo, cowboy, pool-hustler, brawler, miner.' Fits my screen image, don't you think? Eventually, Dempsey fought his way to the top to become the world champion, one of the most colorful men in boxing history—a legend.

"I've done quite a bit of amateur boxing...was a Golden Gloves champion at one time. The past few months I've been in training—just like a fighter training for a big bout—getting in shape for this role. The real Dempsey had his share of romantic encounters. One of his wives was a beautiful actress. So there's material enough for a romance interest—which we'll fictionalize, of course."

"It sounds fabulous."

"Yeah. We're going to begin shooting on location next week—a small town in Nevada where we've built a saloon where Dempsey will have one of his early fights and meet a girl he falls in love with. You're welcome to come along on the set if you like."

"I certainly would!"

"Great. Now I hope you'll excuse me for running off, but I have to fly to San Francisco this afternoon for a conference. My secretary will show you the guest room."

"That's very hospitable of you, but I was planning to get a hotel room—"

"No, no! You'll be my houseguest. I'll be back in the morning and you can fly with me to the Nevada site."

That night, Grant Packer's well-staffed household treated Dusty like an honored guest. She was served a delicious meal and slept in a palatial bedroom.

The excitement and challenge of meeting a famous person like Grant Packer had temporarily taken her mind off her emotional turmoil over Mack. But in the loneliness of the night, after the lights were out, all the feelings rose to the surface. One moment she would be engulfed in heartbreak, then a wave of anger would sweep through her. She had to agree that love and hate were closely related. Half the time she was grieving for Mack; the other half she wanted to kill him. She wasn't sure which desire was the strongest.

The next morning, Dusty was having breakfast on the terrace when Grant Packer put in an appearance. If he'd had a busy night in San Francisco, it wasn't apparent. He looked fresh and full of energy. He greeted Dusty with the same degree of charm and gallantry as he had the day before, then excused himself to make some phone calls. Dusty had just finished breakfast by the time he returned.

"All ready to join me in a flight this morning?"

"Yes. Are we going to the location for your new film?"

"We are. But we're going to take a bit of a side trip."

He kept their destination a mystery. All he would say was that he was going to show her something that would help her in writing the article.

They rode in his chauffeured Rolls to the airport, where his private Lear jet was waiting. When they took off, Dusty had a seat in a plush lounge area where an attendant served her coffee. Packer explained that he had to take care of some paperwork in connection with the film and retired to an office area in the rear section of the plane with his secretary.

Dusty gazed through a window, trying to fathom where they were going. They appeared to be headed east. She saw the Rocky Mountains below, then they veered in a more southerly direction. She saw the winding ribbon of a river; then, far in the distance, a great expanse of blue water.

Grant Packer joined her. "Have you any idea where we're headed?" He smiled, still looking mysterious.

"Let me see if I can made an educated guess. Unless I'm very badly mistaken, that river below us is the Rio Grande and all that blue water up ahead is the Gulf of Mexico. Either you're taking me to South America or we're going to land somewhere on the Texas coast."

Packer laughed, and reached over to give her hand an impetuous squeeze. "You're giving me ideas, Dusty O'Shea. Kidnapping you for a night in South America sounds most appealing."

Careful, she thought warily. He was sending out all kinds of signals that he was starting to enjoy this interview more than he'd expected.

"Pardon my curiosity," he said, "but you write under the byline of Dusty Landers. Is O'Shea your married name?"

"Yes."

He was giving her one of his penetrating gazes. "I notice you're not wearing a wedding ring. Would I be getting too personal if I asked if that has any significance?"

"Why would you want to know?" she parried.

He shrugged. "I suppose, when meeting such an attractive woman, a man is naturally curious about her marital status."

"Well...let's just say it's uncertain at the moment. We're—we're separated."

"I see."

She thought she detected some interest on his part, but he dropped the subject. His gaze, however, lingered on her. "You have unusual coloring, Dusty. The name suits you perfectly. Your skin makes me think of a dusty rose."

She noticed that he was now addressing her by her first name. "My grandmother was a full-blooded Cherokee."

"I see. That explains the large, dark eyes, the hollows of your cheeks under the high cheekbones and the lush black hair. Being in the film industry, I am very much aware of how women look—the structure of a woman's face and her coloring. I see the world's most beautiful actresses all the time. If you don't mind my saying so, Dusty, you have a kind of beauty that is quite uncommon. I can't seem to take my eyes off you."

This was presenting a problem, Dusty thought with a feeling close to panic. She was accustomed to coping with danger, but this was danger of another kind. Flattery from a man like Grant Packer could turn any woman's head. The way he was looking at her would give any female ego a boost. And right now, with her marriage on the rocks, she was dangerously vulnerable.

She made a determined effort to steer the conversation to safer grounds. "You still haven't told me what our destination is."

"Well, I see we're circling to make a landing. Do you recognize the city below us?"

She gazed through the window. "We're very near the coast. I'd say that's Brownsville."

"You're very good at geography, Dusty."

"But why Brownsville? Are you going to shoot some scenes for your film here?"

"No. Let's say I'm going to show you some scenes from a real-life drama."

He would say no more.

The jet came to a smooth landing. A rented limousine was waiting. Obviously Grant's secretary and staff had all the details of this excursion planned. Dusty had the feeling that they kept all the wheels of Grant Packer's life well oiled and running smoothly.

Grant Packer spoke very little as the chauffeured limousine wound through the streets of Brownsville. He appeared lost in private thought. Dusty occupied herself by gazing out the window at the unfolding scenes. When she saw they were approaching the international bridge, she started to feel uncomfortable. Crossing into Mexico stirred wrenching memories. Only a few days before, she had been in this country under other circumstances...with Mack. Crossing the border again so soon was a cruel coincidence—or was it planned? What possible reason, she wondered, would Grant Packer have for bringing her here now?

Asking him appeared to be useless. He had retreated into a fortress of silent contemplation. For some reason beyond her comprehension, he was going to explain himself in his own good time.

The big car crossed smoothly over the bridge. They were stopped on the Mexican side for a perfunctory inspection by Mexican border personnel, then waved on. Soon they were in the streets of Matamoros, Mexico, some so narrow the big car filled them from curb to curb. Dusty deduced that the driver had been briefed before picking them up. He appeared to be following a prearranged course. Grant had not spoken to him once since leaving the airport.

They were moving into what appeared to be a very poor section of the city. The streets were rutted caliche. The limousine crept along, splashing stagnant water from holes in the road. Lining the streets were small houses of the poorest description built of adobe and unpainted boards. Some were little more than sheds covered with rusted tin.

Grant had been slouched down, his face a study in dark contemplation. Suddenly he caught sight of something that made him sit upright. Dusty noticed that his face had flushed. For the first time he spoke to the driver: "Stop here."

Then he turned to Dusty and there was a sudden transformation in his demeanor. He was once again the genial host. "Would you mind if we step out here, Dusty? There is something I want to show you."

He helped her out of the automobile. They were instantly surrounded by a band of ragged, dirty little urchins, their hands outstretched, their faces eager.

Packer thrust his hand in his pocket and tossed a shower of coins to them. He chuckled and tousled the heads of those closest to him. Then he pointed to a poor, two-room dwelling built of adobe bricks crumbling with age. It was surrounded by a broken fence. The small yard was bare, sunbaked dirt, totally barren of even a blade of grass.

"That," Grant Packer said, "was my home from the time I was three years old until I was fourteen."

Dusty was speechless. She realized now the reason for all the mystery about their destination. With his innate flair for theatrical effects, he had planned this little scenario for dramatic shock . . . and he had succeeded.

She knew he had spent his childhood in a Mexican border town. But a thousand words would not have brought home to her the shocking reality of such bitter poverty firsthand.

"I was one of these," he continued, patting one of the ragged children. "I begged coins from the rich American tourists and I shined shoes. I learned the way of the streets. I see myself in their faces." He nodded to the children around them. "We lived in that two-room house, my brother and sister and my mother with her cousin and her three children. There was no plumbing. In the backyard there is an outdoor pit privy. In the summer it was very hot. In the winter it was very cold."

Dusty was momentarily overwhelmed by the anomaly of this tanned, successful Hollywood director and the environment of his childhood. He was attired in a casual imported shirt, slacks and shoes that probably cost more than a laborer in this area earned in a year. Dazed, she shook her head. "And now you are the rich American throwing coins to the poor children."

"Well, I am able to do a bit more than that. Come, I'll show you."

"Just a minute."

By force of habit, Dusty quickly snapped pictures of the neighborhood and caught an excellent mood study of Grant's face as he gazed at his childhood home with a characteristic scowl.

They got back in the car and he gave directions in Spanish to the Mexican-American driver. They drove a few more blocks and came to a large, modern building occupying half a block.

He nodded toward it. "A children's hospital, serving this area. I had it built several years ago and set up a trust fund to keep it going. The patients pay what they can, sometimes a few *centavos*, more often nothing. I thought it was the least I could do after seeing many of my friends die because their parents couldn't afford the most basic medical care. My brother and sister and I were the lucky ones. We were born on the other side of the border. We were American citizens. My mother guarded those birth certificates with her life. She dreamed of the day we could return to a better life."

Dusty took some more pictures.

Then Packer's voice took on a lighter tone. "Enough of this depressing talk. We are now going to have lunch in a restaurant that serves the finest food this side of Mexico City."

It was Dusty's turn to be silent as she digested the morning's events. She was pleased to have been given such a vivid insight into the early background of Grant Packer. At the same time, questions were burning in her mind. Why would a busy actor-director go to such lengths to impress a journalist? Was it a matter of ego? Perhaps he was going out of his way to impress Dusty that he was not the kind of selfish, heartless egomaniac his ex-wife had described. Maybe he was hoping to use Dusty's journalistic skills to set the record straight. Or was there something else motivating him?

When they arrived at the restaurant, a waiter bowed with Latin politeness and showed them to a table. The walls were painted in bright colors. The floors were tiled in glistening mosaic patterns. The tables were set with linen clothes, fine crystal and silver.

"A very elegant place," Dusty observed. "Quite a contrast to your old neighborhood."

"This is a country of great contrasts. Here you are either very poor or very rich. However, these days, even the rich are worried. The inflation has gotten out of hand."

Dusty twisted the stem of her glass thoughtfully, then looked directly at Grant Packer. "Mr. Packer, this trip has been invaluable to me as a writer. But I keep asking myself why you have gone to so much expense and trouble to give me this firsthand look at your childhood."

He suddenly reached across the table, giving her hand a warm clasp that she found strangely unsettling. His deep green eyes searched deeply into hers as a smile played around his lips.

"Couldn't we be less formal? By now we should be good enough friends to be on a first-name basis."

"All right, then. Grant. But you haven't answered my question."

"Yeah, but I will. We'll talk about it over dessert."

Here we go again, Dusty thought with a touch of irritation. The guy loved to play games that kept her guessing. It was part of his ego—part of his style.

Chapter Nine

Packer made only polite, trivial comments during the meal. As they were having coffee with their dessert, he asked, "What do you think of me so far, Dusty O'Shea?"

"I've barely known you twenty-four hours. Don't you think it's a bit early to ask that kind of question?"

"But you must have some first impressions."

Dusty was thoughtful for a moment. "Obviously," she started cautiously, "you are a talented man with a very strong personality. From what you've shown me this morning, I'd say some of what you are was shaped by the struggles of your childhood...a powerful drive to compensate, to overcome the early privations. You appear to have a charitable side that seems to have been overlooked by the media, maybe because of the tough-guy image of your screen character. This is the first I've heard about the children's clinic you've established. Why have you kept that a secret?"

He shrugged. "If I went around bragging about it, the media would say it was a hypocritical gesture on my part to bolster up my public image. After all, I can certainly afford it. With the success of *Backlash*, I'm a millionaire several times over. More important than that, publicity would rob me of some of the personal satisfaction I get out of it. I would feel it was somehow cheapened. This may come as a surprise to you, but my religion tells me that one should not make a public display of charitable acts."

"Yes, I am surprised. You are quite complex. I don't think I'm going to figure out overnight what makes you tick."

He chuckled. "Good. Please don't be in a hurry. I am enjoying your company enormously. Most of the women in my industry are ambitious actresses eaten up by their own egos. They're shallow and narcissistic. You're like a breath of fresh air, Dusty O'Shea. I find your company stimulating in more ways than one."

Dusty suppressed a smile. It was amusing to hear Grant Packer talk in a deprecating manner about anyone else's ego when he had one of the largest egos in Hollywood. But that was not an entirely unattractive quality. His air of self-confidence and self-assurance had a certain charm. He was, simply, secure in the knowledge that he was one of the best. Like his screen heroes, he was larger than life. Whatever else the press might say about him, certainly no one could ever accuse Grant Packer of being a wimp.

"But what do you think of me personally?"

The question caught her off guard. "If I'm going to write about you objectively, I have to keep personal feelings out of it, remember?"

He chuckled. "But it's not possible to be entirely objective about one's feelings where a man and a woman are concerned, is it?"

"Well..." she said slowly, "I find you a gallant, considerate host—"

"Nothing more?"

"You're an interesting man. There are many facets to your personality. I feel I've just scratched the surface."

His green eyes captured hers with their hypnotic, unsettling quality. "On a more basic level, Dusty, do you, as a woman, find me attractive?"

"That's hardly a fair question. Surely you know you are considered one of the most attractive unattached men in America."

"That's flattering, but I noticed you very skillfully ducked giving me your personal assessment."

"You're not going to pin me down. I told you, I'm here to conduct a professional interview with Grant Packer."

"Always the professional."

"Right. Tell me some more about yourself, Grant. What are your interests other than film?"

"Oh, I like to read books on the subjects of history and biography. I lead an active life—skiing, mountain climbing, hiking, sailing."

"You're self-educated."

"Yeah. My formal education ended with high school, except for acting and voice lessons."

"Your first marriage—"

"A disaster. I was young...had just come to Hollywood. Evelyn was some years older, an actress who'd had a few major roles, but was on the way downhill. She took me under her wing; taught me many things about acting and the film industry, for which I was grateful. But she had a drinking problem that kept getting worse. Finally, it got to the point that I couldn't live with her any longer. It was a messy divorce. She never forgave me. She's a very bitter woman and took her venom out on me with that book she wrote about our life together.

"And that brings me around to answering the question you put to me before our lunch. Why did I take the time to go so far out of my way to bring you here? Do you have any guesses?"

"The only reason I can think of is that you would like to counteract all the bad press you've been getting from that book of Evelyn's. You're hoping I'll see a side of you that the tabloids have conveniently overlooked in order to sell copies."

"Yeah, of course, that's obvious. As a matter of fact, I had that in mind when I first agreed to let you do this article. But after meeting you, I've been thinking that I'd like to write an autobiography. Lord knows, I've got the material to make it a bestseller, not only my own career, but all the Hollywood personalities I've rubbed elbows with. Seems like every celebrity is doing the story of their life, these days. Of course, none of them do the actual writing. They collaborate with a professional writer. The public seems to overlook that little fact. I write screenplays, but I wouldn't attempt to write a book. I'll leave that to the professional ability of journalists like yourself. That's your training, just as mine is directing and acting.''

"So, how about it, Dusty O'Shea? How would you like to stick around and do much more than a one-shot article? How would you like to write a book about me? We'll share bylines. I can practically guarantee a bestseller. And I'll be very generous with the division of royalties. I'm not interested so much in the money as I am in seeing the book published. Of course, my ego is involved. I'd like for the world to know the real Grant Packer, those early, hungry years, my dear mother, God rest her soul. Perhaps it's partly for her, partly for the anger I felt toward my old man for deserting us that I want to do the book. I don't know. Call it a catharsis... call it ego. Whatever, it's something I'd like to do and it sure could be profitable to you. What do you say?''

She was stunned. For several moments she was silent, letting this unexpected development soak in. Finally, she said, "I—I don't know what to say. I have to give it a lot of thought. It would mean a drastic change in my plans.''

"Yeah, I would imagine you'd have to spend six months to a year on the project. Naturally, I'd advance any amount of living expenses you'd need while you worked on the book. I'd provide you with an office, a secretary, whatever.''

Dusty shook her head slowly, somewhat dazed. "Well, it's tempting, of course. What journalist wouldn't want a chance to do a book like that? But I also like what I'm doing now... covering news stories around the world....''

"Well, you don't have to make up your mind this minute. Think it over during the next few days while you're doing the magazine piece."

Those "next few days" proved to be interesting and hectic.

After the superb lunch in the Matamoros restaurant, they returned to the Brownsville airport. From there, Grant's jet took them to the small town in Nevada where shooting on the new film was scheduled to begin early in the morning.

It was Dusty's first experience on a movie set. She was awed by the huge amount of equipment. Camera equipment, sound paraphernalia and lights had arrived by the truckload. An eighteen-wheeler as large as a boxcar had been converted into a makeup and dressing room. Another was a traveling cafeteria for the dozens of production crew members, actors and extras.

Dusty kept her camera handy, snapping candid shots of Grant Packer as he moved around the set, giving orders. By the time she was through gathering material for the article, she would have taken hundreds of pictures, from which less than half a dozen would be chosen to illustrate the article.

Watching Grant Packer at work, Dusty could see why some writers had called him a dictator. He was intense and driven, shooting scenes over repeatedly, never satisfied.

Dusty thought he was going to be magnificent in the role of Jack Dempsey. During the week, they filmed the fight scene in the smoky saloon. A crowd of shouting, perspiring extras jammed around an improvised ring. Grant, in the role of a young, tough

Jack Dempsey, faced an opponent who was bigger, meaner and more experienced.

Dusty watched the scene from a balcony, astounded by the realism. Packer and his opponent, who was, in reality, a stuntman who had been a professional boxer, battled while the crowd shoved, yelled and waved fistfuls of money, making bets.

There was the smack of leather against flesh, the grunting of the fighters, the shouts and curses of the crowd. Grant Packer's body glistened with sweat. His powerful muscles rippled as he circled his opponent in the famous Jack Dempsey crouch, then lashed out with lightning fast punches. It was a role that suited his screen image—the tough barroom brawler.

So realistic was the scene that Dusty momentarily forgot she was watching a movie being filmed. It was as if she had been transported by a time warp to a bygone era before the U.S. entered World War I, when the real Jack Dempsey was battling his way around the tank-town circuit on his way to becoming a world champion.

She forgot the cameras and the lighting. Not until the assistant director yelled, "Cut—that's a print," was she jerked with a start back to reality.

Late that afternoon, there was a knock on the door of her motel room. Grant Packer stood there, his broad shoulders filling a tweed sport coat. There was a purple bruise under one eye.

"Well, Dusty, what did you think of today's scenes?"

"Fantastic. You guys weren't pulling your punches, were you?"

He fingered the bruise and winced. "Not as much as I'd like. We were trying to be realistic."

"You certainly succeeded. You had me convinced. You'll have audiences on the edge of their seats. It looks to me like you're going to have another winner—maybe even bigger than *Backlash*."

"Suppose we see how it's looking on film. Some early rushes are ready."

He escorted her to one of the big trucks, which had been converted into a viewing room.

They sat in the dark as a projector flashed scenes on a screen. There were close-ups of Grant Packer's rugged features, some action shots of the fight from different angles and some rough cuts of the leading lady meeting Dempsey for the first time.

"It looks really good," Dusty said when the lights went on.

"Yeah, well, it'll do once the cutting room gets through with it."

They walked outside. The sky was turning red with a brilliant desert sunset. The winter air was sharp and dry. Dusty drew her trench coat closer against the chill.

"I'll buy you supper," Grant offered.

"Okay."

"Not here. I want to fly into Las Vegas. We can be there in forty-five minutes."

She nodded. "All right."

"What do you like? Chinese? Italian?"

She grinned. "Do you really want to know?"

"Sure. It's my treat. I want you to enjoy the meal."

"Okay. If you really want to know, I love junk food. Give me a McDonald's hamburger and a milk shake and I'm in heaven."

He grinned. "A lady after my own heart. How about a pizza with root beer and top it off with a banana split?"

She rolled her eyes. "My mouth is watering. Or *chalupas* and enchiladas."

He made a face. "No thanks. I never want to look another tamale in the face. How about some of the colonel's fried chicken topped off with a box of chocolate cookies?"

"Now you're talking."

He laughed. "How do you manage to stay so slim on a diet like that?"

"Just lucky, I guess."

"Well, what'll it be tonight?"

"Hard to decide. Let me see... I think I'm in the mood for a pizza with a banana split for dessert."

"All right. I'll buy you a pizza and the biggest banana split in Las Vegas. How does that sound?"

"Like you just talked yourself into company for the evening."

Grant's private jet, waiting at a landing strip near the small town, flew them smoothly to Las Vegas. They were accompanied by two large men who Dusty learned were Grant's bodyguards. When they arrived in Las Vegas, a cab took them to one of the largest casino hotels on the strip. They had no sooner stepped from the cab than Grant was recognized and surrounded by fans who pushed and shoved to get to him. They were warded off by the two burly bodyguards as

Grant and Dusty hurried into the hotel. On the way, Grant good-naturedly signed some autographs.

It was a new experience for Dusty. Until now, when she had anything to do with celebrities, she had been in the crowd, battling to get close enough to get a statement or take a picture. It was nice, for a change, to be on the inside track.

Once inside the hotel, they were greeted profusely by the management and escorted to a table where they had some privacy. One of the casino owners, alerted that Grant Packer was on the premises, came down to personally greet the actor. "When are you going to do that show for us, Grant?"

"When you pay me enough money." Grant grinned.

"We don't make that much money. Anything else we can do for you?"

"Yes, I promised this little lady a pizza with anchovies and olives, a glass of root beer and the biggest banana split in Las Vegas."

"Then you came to the right place. If we can't make it here, we'll send out for it." The owner snapped a finger at a waiter hovering nearby. "How about you, Grant?"

"The pizza sounds good to me. But I'll have a glass of real beer with it."

The casino owner gave Dusty a curious look. "You look very familiar, young lady. Are you in show business?"

She laughed. "Hardly."

"She's pretty enough to be the leading lady, isn't she?" Grant said. "This is Dusty O'Shea, a journalist. She's doing an article about me."

"Of course!" the casino owner exclaimed. "I knew I'd seen you somewhere. You were on the news a week or so ago. That must have been some hellish experience. But you seemed so cool in that interview."

"I was scared spitless," Dusty said. "It just didn't show."

The casino owner shook his head. "I don't know when this terrorism is going to stop. Listen, anything you want while you're here, just ask."

Once he left them alone, they chatted about the picture Grant was shooting. Then the meal arrived and Dusty eagerly tasted a slice of the pizza.

"How is it?" Grant asked.

"Umm," she murmured, rolling her eyes in an expression of ecstasy.

But as she ate, she began to grow sad. Her appetite faded. She laid the remains of the slice on her plate, staring at it miserably.

"Something wrong with the pizza?" Grant asked.

"No. It's delicious."

"Then why'd you stop eating?"

Dusty blinked quickly, fighting back tears. "It's silly. Forgive me."

"No. Tell me. If there's something wrong with the pizza I want to send it back."

"It has nothing to do with the pizza. It's just that—well... I suddenly thought about my husband. He's always fussing at me about junk food. For a minute I thought I could hear him telling me I ought to be eating vegetables and fresh fruit."

Grant gazed at her thoughtfully. "It takes a while to get over somebody."

"Yes, it does."

"Do you think your marriage can be patched up?"

Dusty shook her head, trying hard not to cry. She swallowed with difficulty. "It's a hopeless situation."

Grant held her hand. With his free hand, he smoothed back the hair from her temple with surprising gentleness for such a rough-looking man. It was nice to be comforted. Tonight she felt very lonely and sad.

In the following days, Dusty realized she was seeing more and more of Grant Packer. Whenever he wasn't busy on the set, he arranged one way or another to be with her. One day when there was a break in the shooting, he asked her to fly to San Francisco with him. He said he had business there, but once they arrived, he spent his time with her. They rode the cable cars, ate at the Hyatt Regency and wandered through Chinatown, where Grant bought her a beautiful jade necklace.

On the weekend, they flew to the coast and spent the day on Grant's yacht, a beautiful vessel large enough to sail anywhere in the world.

They were on deck, watching a spectacular Pacific sunset, when Grant turned to her, his eyes serious and thoughtful. "Have you thought any more about my biography?"

"Yes, I've given it a lot of thought. It's a very tempting offer."

There were several moments of silence as Grant continued to look at her thoughtfully. Then he said slowly, "Dusty, we haven't known each other very long, but I've grown to care a great deal for you. Two busted marriages have left me very gun-shy. I didn't think I'd ever feel this way again. But you're so dif-

ferent from the other women I meet. The thought of
your leaving makes me very unhappy. I want to keep
you around. We could have a lot of fun together.
When I finish shooting *Dempsey*, I'm going to sail
down to Acapulco for a few days. Then I'm going to
Alaska for several weeks to shoot a TV special. After
that, my plans are to start a film on location in Ja-
pan. I'd like to think you'd want to go with me."

Dusty was so surprised it took her a moment to
gather her thoughts. "As your biographer or your
girlfriend?"

"I'm hoping maybe both."

She couldn't decipher her own emotions at that
point. She felt pleased and confused, happy and sad,
thrilled and frightened. "Grant, you're one of the
most interesting and attractive men I've ever met. I—
I don't know what to say. Of course I'm flattered that
you'd feel that way about me. A man like you could
have the pick of the most beautiful women in Hollywood. I guess at this point I don't know my own mind.
I'm still broken up over Mack...."

He grasped her hand, his sea-green eyes searching
hers. "I don't want to rush you, Dusty. You could just
hang around the way you've been doing, starting to
work on my biography. We could take it slow and easy
and let things develop. I think in time you'll feel the
way I do."

Dusty struggled with her conflicting emotions. "It's
a big decision. I'll have to make up my mind if I want
to drop all my other commitments and spend the next
six months or a year working on your biography. I
have other assignments I'd have to cancel. It would be
a drastic change in my career. Give me a few more

days. I'm going to have to do a lot of soul-searching, Grant...."

On the one hand, she thought, Grant Packer was offering her exactly the kind of excitement and travel she craved. True, she'd be temporarily giving up her photojournalism activities, but in their place would be a life of glamour and excitement as the companion of one of the most attractive celebrities in America. What woman in her right mind wouldn't be thrilled at that? Still she hesitated. Grant Packer, as macho and attractive as he was, was not Mack O'Shea....

Two nights later, Dusty was in her motel room typing the final draft of her article when she took a break to watch the national news. One of the items caught her attention. A high-ranking executive in the Nicholson Corporation had been kidnapped in a South American country and was being held for a two-million-dollar ransom.

Shortly after the broadcast, Dusty's phone rang. It was Myra. "Did you catch tonight's news?"

"Yes."

"That oil executive that's been kidnapped—isn't that the Dallas company that Mack went to work for?"

"Yes, it is."

"There's a big story brewing there, Dusty. I just got a call from a news editor who has an inside source on the situation. Now, this is very hush-hush, but according to his source, the owner of the oil company, Bob Nicholson, who also happens to be one of the richest men in America, is putting together a private

SWAT team to fly down to South America and rescue the guy.''

"Wow!"

"I'll say, 'wow.' Can you see the potential? This editor wants you on the story. What do you think? How are you coming on the Grant Packer piece?''

"I'm typing the final draft right now. But why am I getting this South American assignment?''

"You're a big name in the field these days, my friend. You had a good reputation before, and after all the publicity you got on that skyjacking, your byline is worth big bucks.''

Dusty shook her head slowly. "I—I don't know, Myra...."

"What do you mean, you don't know? I thought you'd jump at a chance like this.''

"Well, there have been some unexpected developments here.'' She paused, hunting for the right words. "I've had an offer from Grant Packer that's hard to refuse. He wants me to collaborate with him on a biography, a book about his life and career. He's made me a very generous offer. If I accept it would mean giving up all my other assignments for six months to a year.''

There was a surprised silence. Finally, Myra exclaimed, "Now it's my time to say wow.''

"Yeah. I knew you'd be bowled over.''

"Now you're talking real big bucks!''

Dusty smiled at the excitement in her agent's voice. "Myra, before you start calculating your ten percent of a bestseller, I haven't definitely decided to do it.''

"What's to decide? How can you turn down a deal like that?''

"Well, there are complications."

"Such as?"

Dusty felt her face growing warm. "They're personal."

Another surprised silence. Then, with a note of awe, Myra said, "Dusty, do you mean . . . Grant Packer . . . you and Grant Packer?" Her voice went several notes up the scale with each word.

"Now don't jump to a lot of conclusions—"

"Yeah, but Grant Packer. I mean, when I see that man on the screen, I get hot flashes. So do most of the women in America. And you're right there with him and you and he are . . . are . . ."

"Myra, we're not having an affair, so calm down. At least not yet. But . . . well . . . yeah, he is interested in me. If I did the book, I'd travel with him. There's no offer of marriage involved. You know these Hollywood types. He's been burned twice and he's in no hurry to go that route again. Still, we've been together a lot. He's told me he cares for me and wants me to be with him all the time. That adds up to live-in girlfriend, in Hollywood language."

"Whatever the language, it adds up to one hell of a romance. Well, I'll call the editor and tell him to get somebody else for the South American kidnap thing—"

"Now, don't be too hasty. I didn't say I was accepting Grant's offer."

"How can you turn it down? You're still breathing, aren't you? Look, this guy is offering you exactly the kind of life you thrive on—travel, excitement. You'd be surrounded by celebrities, jetting all over the world with a movie star. And while all that is going on, you're putting your byline as collaborator on a book that's sure to be a bestseller. Why, I can hear the publishers now!''

''Myra, you know I haven't gotten over Mack yet. I'm not ready to become involved with another man. Sure, Grant is one of the most charming, most attractive men I've ever run into. At times, I'm very tempted. But then Mack gets in the way. I'm still in love with him. I wish I weren't. It would make things a lot easier. But that's how it is. I have the feeling I've gotten into a situation here over my head and I don't know how to extricate myself. This South American assignment might give me an out. At least, it would give me an excuse to get away from here for a while so I could get my head straight.''

''Well, if that's how you feel...'' Myra replied reluctantly.

''The only problem is if I accept this assignment, it could mean I'd be thrown together with Mack again. Do you have any idea who Bob Nicholson is hiring for this undercover team?''

''None whatsoever. The whole thing is a closely guarded secret, naturally. He doesn't want the justice department down on his back. So far the news media has been stonewalled in any attempt to get inside information. This leak I told you about is all we have to go on. We don't even know for sure if it's reliable information, though it's supposed to come from a pretty good source.''

''If they're putting together an undercover team, there's a good chance Mack will be on it. Do you suppose that's the real reason your editor friend wants to hire me—thinking I could use my relationship with Mack to get on the inside track?''

"The thought did occur to me, but I'm not sure if he's aware that your husband is working for Bob Nicholson."

"My estranged husband," Dusty corrected with a sigh. "Myra, you don't know of some assignment that would take me to China, do you? If I stay here, I have to cope with Grant Packer. If I accept the South American assignment, I might run smack dab into Mack again. Either way, I lose."

"Well, I guess you could just take a vacation."

"No," she said slowly, shaking her head. "I have to keep working."

There was a moment of silence while Dusty wrestled with her conflicting emotions.

"All right. I'll take the assignment."

Chapter Ten

When Dusty arrived in Dallas, she met a stone wall at every corporate level of the Nicholson Corporation. At the top of the ladder, Bob Nicholson would see no one without an appointment and he wasn't giving out appointments. Dusty could not get past his secretary.

For several days, she haunted the offices at the Nicholson building in downtown Dallas, going from office to office, trying to see various officers from vice presidents to public-relations people, without success.

The building was swarming with reporters. No one was able to pierce the veil of secrecy. They had to content themselves with periodic press releases handed out by the public-relations department, which gave very little beyond the initial news story that a company vice president had been kidnapped in South America. The company was negotiating with the kidnappers, who were demanding two million dollars in ransom.

"So far, I'm wasting my time and your editor's expense money," Dusty said when she reported her lack of progress to her agent.

"Nobody else seems to be doing any better," Myra reassured her.

"How about this inside source you told me about?"

"We keep hoping he'll break his silence. So far, nothing more has been heard from him."

"Do you have any hint about who he might be?"

"None whatever. We think it has to be someone on the inside, but why he'd want to tip off this particular editor, we don't know. Could be he has some kind of grudge against the company and wanted to irritate them by spilling the beans. Whatever his reason, he's apparently gotten cold feet and decided to clam up."

"Well, it's useless to try to get through to any of the officers. In situations like this I've found out if you can't get to the top, sometimes you can get somewhere at the bottom. Tomorrow I'm going to try the janitor."

"Good idea." Myra hesitated, then asked, "Have you run into Mack?"

"No. I'm afraid any minute I'm going to bump into him somewhere in the building, but I haven't seen him. Come to think of it, that's kind of strange. Maybe he's already taken off for South America."

That thought gave Dusty a chill. Sending a private commando squad down to South America to tackle a band of armed kidnappers was dangerous business.

The next morning she wandered down a stairway in the Nicholson building. In a basement room, she found a maintenance man piling trash into a compactor.

"Hi," she said, smiling. "I guess I got lost. I was looking for an exit to the parking garage."

The worker, a young man with a bushy mop of straggly blond hair, dressed in a blue shirt and jeans, paused to wipe his sleeve across his perspiring forehead. "You came down one too many floors. You got to back up to the ground level and go out through the lobby."

"Thanks." She gave him a dazzling smile. "I'm not very bright about finding my way around."

He gave her another look, then leaned against the trash compactor, apparently in no hurry to get back to work.

"Yeah, well, it's easy to get lost in a big building like this."

"Have you worked here long?"

"Six months. Trying to save enough bread to go back to college."

"Oh. SMU?"

"Yeah."

"What are you majoring in?"

"Computers. That's where the money is these days. You can't run a computer, you might as well forget it."

"That's the truth. Listen, is there a cold-drink machine around here anywhere? I'm dying of thirst."

"There's one on the landing. Turn right down the hall. You'll see it."

"Thanks. Can I bring you something? You look hot and thirsty."

"Well, yeah, thanks. I'd like a Coke."

"Be right back."

Dusty found, to her delight, not only a soft-drink machine but a snack dispenser. She dropped coins in the slot, getting two soft drinks, several candy bars and a package of chocolate cookies.

She went back down the stairs and handed one of the drinks to the young maintenance man.

"Candy bar?" she offered.

"No, thanks. Bad for my acne."

"I just can't pass up a snack machine. Guess I'm hooked on junk food. I love this kind of chocolate bar with almonds."

Dusty devoured the candy bar and sipped her soft drink. "Oh, my name is Dusty O'Shea."

"Pleased to meet you. I'm Jim Flannigan."

"Nice to make your acquaintance, Jim. Do you like working for the Nicholson Corporation?"

"It's all right. They treat their people pretty good—decent salary and benefits."

"Too bad about the company vice president getting kidnapped," she said casually.

"Yeah." He nodded.

"Did you know him?"

"Nah. Those big shots stay in the penthouse offices. Anyway, he didn't work here. He was with the operation down in South America."

"Oh. I guess his family is terribly worried. I heard the kidnappers want two million dollars. D'you suppose the company is going to pay his ransom?"

The man shrugged. "Old man Nicholson could probably take it out of petty cash and never miss it. But the scuttlebutt I hear around the personnel is that they don't think the kidnappers would let the guy live once they get the money. Those ain't just ordinary kidnappers. They've got some kind of political ax to grind.''

"I see. Gee, that looks pretty bad for the guy."

"Yeah, well, maybe they can save him. They're going to try something."

Dusty immediately tensed, but was careful to keep her voice casual. She took another bite of her candy bar. "What are they going to try?"

"I don't know exactly. But I worked the night shift last night. There was this van come into the parking garage. A half-dozen guys piled out of it, dressed in those kind of camouflaged fatigues hunters and soldiers wear. I was sweeping in the parking garage when they parked the van. When the door opened, I saw a bunch of guns in there. And I don't think they'd been hunting. You don't go hunting with automatic weapons and that's what I saw in the van."

"Gee. Sounds exciting. Real undercover stuff. What do you think they were doing?"

"Practicing. Getting in shape. I heard them talking about it as they got out of the van. See, the company owns this ranch about thirty miles from town. They use it for entertaining big shots in the oil business. Last fall, they had a big company picnic out there and I got to see it. That's how I know about it. That's where they'd been, all right. They call the place the Nicholson Oil Patch. I heard them mention it as they were leaving the van."

"Well...but how did you know those guys you saw getting out of the van last night were Nicholson people?"

"They had a key to the building. Walked right in and took the elevator upstairs. Besides, old man Nicholson was with them. I spotted him as soon as they got out of the van. They didn't pay any attention to me. I was some distance away, sweeping. I don't think they even saw me."

"Real cloak-and-dagger stuff, huh?"

"Yeah." The young maintenance man grinned. "Just like in that Grant Packer movie, *Backlash*."

Dusty was struggling to mask her excitement. She licked the chocolate from her fingers and dropped her empty soft-drink can in a nearby garbage can. "Well, I've got to run along. Good luck with your computer classes, Jim."

"Yeah. I'm not going to spend my life pushing brooms. Computers. That's where it's at."

"Right."

Dusty trotted back up the stairs and hurried through the lobby to the parking garage where she had left her rented car.

Soon she was on a freeway headed north. Before leaving the city limits, she took an exit off the freeway and called the Nicholson Corporation from a service-station phone booth. When the Nicholson switchboard operator answered, Dusty said, "Baker Delivery Service here. We have a package to deliver to the Nicholson Oil Patch. Can you tell us how to get there?"

The switchboard operator obliged her with clear directions. In minutes, Dusty was back on the freeway, speeding north.

After a half hour, she took an exit and followed a maze of farm roads. Soon, she was out in Texas prai-

rie country that was covered with brush and scrubby
mesquite. A turn took her off the paved hardtop onto
a gravel road. On either side were barbed-wire fences.
She was getting into a remote area. She hadn't passed
another car or seen a living person for miles. Then she
saw a gate and a sign, Nicholson Oil Patch.

But the gate was locked, and on the other side a van
was parked. A man dressed in a Western hat and boots
was sitting in a chair tilted against the side of the van.
He was reading a magazine. Beside him, leaning
against the van, was a double-barreled shotgun. Obviously, the Nicholson people did not have the welcome mat out for visitors.

The man looked up from his magazine and stared at
Dusty as she drove past. She did not slow down, but
continued down the road until she drove around a
bend and was out of sight of the guard. Then she
pulled to the shoulder of the road and switched off her
engine. She slung her camera bag over a shoulder and
walked across the road to the barbed-wire fence
marking the boundary of the Nicholson ranch. There
were numerous posted signs warning that trespassers
would be prosecuted.

Dusty passed her camera bag ahead of her between
the strands of barbed wire. She found a stick, which
she thrust between two strands of the wire, forcing
them apart as far as possible. Then she eased her way
between the vicious, sharp barbs.

Safely inside the fence, she picked up her bag and
headed into the brush. It was one of those sunny days
with temperatures in the high seventies that warm the
Texas scrubland between winter northers. Dusty followed a cow path that wound among clumps of cac-

tus, brush and scrubby trees, all bristling with thorns. She reasoned that a cow path would eventually lead her to the corrals and feed barns.

Her plan proved to be correct. After following the path for a half hour, she came to an opening in the brush, through which she could see ranch buildings. She fitted a five-hundred-millimeter telephoto mirror lens on one of her cameras and gazed through the viewfinder. She saw a sprawling white ranch house and several smaller buildings, a swimming pool, a tennis court and a landing strip with a hangar and a wind sock. On the landing strip was a private jet, its metallic fuselage gleaming in the bright sunlight.

Elegant spread, she thought. But why not? Nicholson, one of the richest men in America could well afford it.

Suddenly, her thoughts were shattered. Her breath caught in her throat and she went rigid. The cold, round circle of a rifle muzzle was pressed against the back of her neck.

"Just sit real still, ma'am," a masculine voice behind her rumbled. "Now put that camera down and stand up slow like. Don't make no sudden moves. I'd hate to have to shoot a lady this early in the day."

Dusty swallowed hard and obeyed the command.

"Now, ma'am, let's take a stroll down to the big house. I reckon the boss is going to be kinda curious about how come you're trespassing on his property. I'd say you're in a mite of trouble."

Dusty turned slowly. She saw that her captor was a tall, lanky man wearing cowboy boots, jeans and a checkered shirt. His face was tanned the color of saddle leather. His Winchester rifle was in the crook of his arm, the muzzle pointed toward the ground now, but she knew he could swing it up and pull the trigger faster than she could blink an eye.

She was frightened, but at the same time elated. Nicholson wouldn't be posting a guard at the gate and having his ranch patrolled unless he had some kind of top-secret activity going on here. The young maintenance man's hunch must be right—this was where Nicholson was training his private SWAT team.

"Gee, I didn't know I was trespassing," she said, trying to look innocent. "I was out bird-watching. Guess I got lost and . . ."

The man with the rifle gave her a baleful stare. "Bird-watching? Well, let's go down and talk to one of the bosses about it." He motioned with his rifle for her to start walking.

She put her camera in her bag and obeyed.

They crossed the ranch yard and entered the front door of the main building. Her captor took his hat off and pointed to a room off to the right of a long hallway.

The room appeared to be a kind of study. Bookshelves lined one wall. Another wall was covered with large maps. Dusty's quick eye noted that they were maps of South America.

A man seated behind a desk was dressed in the kind of camouflaged jump suit that hunters wear. He glanced up from papers spread before him on the desk.

"Colonel Sawyer, I caught this young lady in the brush, taking pictures of the ranch house. Claims she was out bird-watching and got lost."

The man named Sawyer rose, an angry scowl on his face. He was a large, burly man with big, scarred hands. "Who are you?" he demanded. "What the hell are you doing spying on this place?"

"Honest, I don't know why everybody's so upset," Dusty said. "I didn't know I was trespassing. You see, I belong to this bird-watching society and we think there's an ivory-billed woodpecker in this area. At least that's what Miss Towers claims. She's the president of our bird-watching society. She's a librarian and everybody thinks she's an authority on birds. I'm not so sure she knows as much as she claims to know, but anyway, she insists she spotted this ivory-billed woodpecker, which is supposed to be nearly extinct and nobody has ever seen one on the North American continent in thirty years, so you can see how thrilled we would be if we actually did see one here, but you have to verify something that important, like reports from two or three bird-watchers verifying what she saw, otherwise—"

"Wait a minute! I swear, lady, you can talk more than my wife. And can that guff about bird-watching. I don't believe a word of it. Slim, here, says he caught you taking pictures of the ranch house. The ranch house is not a woodpecker. I want the truth out of you. I want to know who you are and what you're up to."

Dusty looked wide-eyed and innocent. "I just told you . . . I was bird-watching. There's this very rare woodpecker, you see—"

She was interrupted when the door to her right opened. She turned and gasped.

Mack O'Shea stood in the doorway. He was speechless. His mouth was slightly agape as he stared at her with an expression of stunned surprise.

Chapter Eleven

Dusty!" Mack exclaimed, when he was able to speak.

Sawyer looked from Dusty to Mack with a puzzled frown. "Do you know this woman, Mack?"

He nodded, still dazed and baffled. "Yes, I know her. She's my wife."

"Your wife!" Sawyer exploded.

There was a moment of silence while Sawyer digested this surprising bit of information. "Is she really a bird-watcher?"

"A what?"

"Bird-watcher. She said she's a bird-watcher looking for a woodpecker."

Mack glared at Dusty. "How did you come up with that? You wouldn't know a woodpecker from a buzzard."

She looked sheepish and shrugged. "Best I could come up with on the spur of the moment."

Sawyer scowled again. "Well, if she's not out bird-watching, what the hell is she doing here, snooping around with a camera?"

"I don't know, but I'm sure going to find out."

Mack grabbed her arm and pulled her roughly with him through the doorway. "You come with me."

Dusty's emotions had gone into a tailspin upon seeing Mack again. Ever since returning to Dallas, she had braced herself against the possibility of running into Mack, trying to be prepared for the inevitable. But all that had not helped much, now that the confrontation was a reality. Hurt, sadness, anger, longing, despair all cascaded through her in a wrenching torrent. A part of her longed for Mack to take her in his arms, to kiss her and soothe her feelings, to tell her that he had changed and everything was going to be the way it used to be, while another part of her felt a rising tide of anger at his stubbornness, which had torn them apart.

To cover her demoralized state, she kept up an air of bravado, her chin high, her gaze level.

Mack took her with him into another room that looked like a den. It was furnished with a couch, comfortable chairs, a bar, TV, bookshelves and stereo. In spite of her emotional upheaval over Mack, Dusty's sharp eyes noted that here, as in the other room, there were large maps of South America on the wall.

Mack sat her in a straight-backed chair facing him and he leaned against a table, his arms crossed. His face was stern, but Dusty saw other things in his eyes.

She thought that he, too, was experiencing powerful emotions at seeing her again.

But whatever he was feeling, he kept it to himself. His voice was as stern as his expression. "All right, Dusty. Explanation time."

"You don't believe the bird-watching story?"

"Don't insult my intelligence," he said impatiently.

"I had car trouble and wandered in here looking for a telephone."

"I don't believe that, either. What I can't understand is how you turned up here. From what I've been reading in the papers, you're all tied up with your new boyfriend, Grant Packer, in California. I'm surprised he let you out of his sight."

"My new boyfriend?"

"Don't lie about that, too," he said bitterly.

She suddenly understood that Mack's anger wasn't entirely over her stumbling on this clandestine paramilitary operation. She and Grant had been seen together on several occasions. It was a hot item, which the tabloids had immediately grabbed. She had seen one of the headlines: "Grant Packer in Love Spin over Lady Journalist." At the time it had only amused her. She hadn't thought that Mack might see it. Obviously he had, or had seen one like it.

"Do you think Grant Packer and I are having an affair?"

"What else am I supposed to think?"

"I don't suppose anything I'd say would make any difference if you've already got your mind made up."

"Probably not."

She tried to gauge Mack's feelings. "Jealous?" she asked lightly.

"Of course not," he said coldly. "You made your decision when you went on to California instead of trying to work out our problem. I could see that you had no intention of trying to save our marriage."

"What are you talking about, Mack O'Shea?" she gasped furiously. "I talked myself blue that night in Monterrey when you made it perfectly clear you weren't going to compromise an inch. Either I change my life-style to suit you, or forget it. Well, I had to go on to California. I had an assignment to fulfill. As for me and Grant Packer, I didn't see *you* sitting around pining. The last message I had on my answering machine was that you were taking Laura Nicholson out to dinner. You've probably been seeing more of her than I was of Grant Packer."

"I doubt that," he said, his voice even colder. "From what I've been reading, you're about to become Grant Packer's newest live-in girlfriend, if you haven't already."

"Do you believe everything you read?"

"I don't know. Should I?"

She weighed her answer, angry enough to let him think the worst.

"How about you and Laura Nicholson? Have you taken up where you left off?"

"Under the circumstances, I don't think that's any concern of yours."

Sudden pain wrenched at her heart. They were like two strangers. She was furious with him and at the same time she grieved for the closeness they had once shared.

With a determined effort, she put a cap on her personal feelings and took refuge in her professionalism. She suddenly fired a question at him, hoping to catch him off guard. "When are you leaving for South America?"

His eyes narrowed. "What gives you the idea I'm going to South America?"

"You're training a commando squad here, aren't you?"

"Who gave you that kind of information?"

"You know I can't reveal my sources."

He looked exasperated. "We have an iron-tight lid of security on this operation. I'm going to find out who's leaking information, and when I do, heads are going to roll. Somebody is going to get fired."

"You'll never find out from me."

He gave her a thoughtful look. "No, I don't suppose we will."

At that point, the door opened and a man entered the room. Dusty recognized Bob Nicholson at once. He was a tall, slender man with silver-gray hair. He nodded to Mack, then directed his attention to Dusty.

Mack straightened up from his position leaning against the table. "Bob. I don't think you've ever met my wife, Dusty. Dusty, this is my friend and employer, Bob Nicholson."

"How do you do, Mrs. O'Shea," Nicholson said in a warm, gracious tone. "I just came from Jack Sawyer's office. He told me you were here." He turned to Mack with a questioning expression.

"I want to warn you, Bob," Mack said, "Dusty is not here on a social visit. She is a professional journalist."

"Yes, I'm aware of that." He turned his gaze back to Dusty. "Am I to understand you are here to get a news story, Mrs. O'Shea?"

"Is there a news story here?" Dusty countered.

A thoughtful smile played around Nicholson's lips. "Who told you about this place, Mrs. O'Shea?"

Her only reply was a silent shrug.

Mack interjected, "You're wasting your breath, Bob. You can hang her up by her thumbs and she won't reveal her sources. She can be very stubborn."

Dusty shot Mack a dirty look.

Nicholson smiled. "Well, we're hardly going to do anything as drastic as hang you up by your thumbs, Mrs. O'Shea, though I have to admit, I'm disturbed that anyone could find out about this. This is a very delicate situation. I thought we were maintaining extremely tight security."

"There're always cracks in any security measures."

"Apparently," Nicholson agreed dryly. "I wonder how many reporters have found out as much as you seem to have discovered."

"At the present time, nobody else, as far as I know."

He moved to a window, and silently gazed outside for several minutes as if deep in thought. Then he turned. "I'm going to be very frank with you, Mrs. O'Shea. Obviously, you already have pretty well figured out what we're up to. Yes, we've gotten together a half-dozen people like Mack, here, who've had police or military experience. They're all experts in their fields. One man is a demolitions expert, another skilled in communications. We even have a woman test pilot who can fly anything from a jet to a helicopter.

Two of our people are Vietnam veterans. Another, like Mack, is ex-CIA. One was with the police SWAT team and another worked for the FBI for several years. You already met Colonel Jack Sawyer. He's a tough, experienced retired army officer, something of a soldier of fortune. He was with the Israeli military for several years on some type of secret antiterrorist operation. Jack will command our group. We feel very fortunate in securing his expertise. For the past week, we've been here on the ranch, practicing some maneuvers and working out plans. We intend to go to South America, find out where the kidnappers are holding Emory Wilson and free him.''

Dusty listened, fascinated by the incredible drama. ''You've been telling the media that you're negotiating with the kidnappers.''

''We are. And I'm willing to pay the two million dollars for his freedom. But now they're making other demands. They want the release of a large number of political prisoners being held by the South American country. We're coming to believe that the ransom money is only incidental to the kidnappers' motivation, which is more political than financial.''

''Is the government down there going to cooperate?''

Nicholson smiled ruefully. ''No. They are not going to free the political prisoners. And the police down there are not going to be very effective in solving this case. They have their hands full elsewhere. The country has been racked by civil strife. There is street fighting—mobs that want to overthrow the president. It's a toss-up as to whether the army is going to remain loyal to the president or go over to the other side, in which case the present government will topple. The hero of the revolutionary movement is a man named Juan Allisto, *El Hombre*, they call him. He's a kind of small-time Fidel Castro, beard and all.

"The U.S. embassy down there isn't able to help us much. They're in the process of packing up to leave, as are the embassies of other countries. So you can see, it's a pretty dismal situation. The kidnapping of one American businessman has been lost and ignored in the general civil turmoil. Our fear is that with all this going on, Emory could be murdered and no one down there would give it a second thought."

"So you've decided to take the law into your own hands and launch a private commando raid to locate and free Emory Wilson."

"Something like that."

"Do you have any idea where the kidnappers are holding him?"

"At the present time, none whatever. That will be our first task when we get to South America."

"How do you expect to get your people and your equipment into the country? Seems like the government down there would be a little reluctant to let a private army cross their borders with an uprising on their hands."

"Yes, that is a problem. It is very difficult to book air passage down there. Flights are erratic and uncertain. Now let me explain why I am telling you all this, Mrs. O'Shea."

He slowly paced the room, gathering his thoughts. When he spoke, it was in a low, grave tone. "First of all, you're obviously a sharp, professional investigative journalist or you wouldn't have gotten this far.

You'd soon have the rest of the story anyway. But I'm putting my cards on the table in the hopes that we can appeal to your sense of moral obligation not to publish any of this for the time being. Emory Wilson, besides being a valued company official, is a lifelong friend of mine. He's a fine gentleman, a family man with two children. I'd do anything to get him back here safely. If it meant paying the two million dollars, I'd do it without a second thought. But as you see, it's become more complicated than that. We just can't sit here while Emory is used as a political pawn and eventually murdered by political terrorists. We have to do something."

For the first time, Nicholson's calm, dignified demeanor wavered and his voice trembled. "If you give this story to the press now, it would destroy our chances. Our hope is to slip into the country quietly in the guise of tourists and catch the kidnappers off guard. But if the media publish our plans, the kidnappers would be alerted. They might even kill Emory. Do you want that on your conscience?"

Dusty shook her head slowly, sobered by the responsibility. She drew a deep breath. "It's a hell of a story, but you've put me in quite a spot, Mr. Nicholson. No," she said quietly, "I won't break the story. You have my word."

Nicholson sighed with relief. He looked as if a great weight had been lifted from him. "I trust you, Mrs. O'Shea. And I thank you."

"How about letting me go along with you to South America? At least I'd be on the spot when you pull your commando raid. Maybe I'd get a scoop there."

Nicholson rubbed his chin thoughtfully. "I—I don't know. That country is a powder keg. It would be very dangerous. However, I'm going to leave that up to your husband. Mack, you can do whatever you think best. I have to get back to the office."

Nicholson took both of Dusty's hands in his, giving them a warm squeeze as he bowed slightly. "It has been a pleasure meeting you, Mrs. O'Shea. And again, you have my deepest gratitude for keeping the security on this operation intact."

"He's a nice man," Dusty said, after he had left. "I can see why you like him. Now, when do we leave for South America?"

"I'm leaving in a few days. You're not going anywhere."

Her eyes narrowed. "What do you mean by that?"

"Exactly what I said. This is an undercover, military-type operation. It's going to be dangerous. The last thing we need in this kind of touchy situation is a journalist running around taking pictures. Besides, you might get your fool self shot."

"Would you care if I did?"

He didn't reply.

"Well," she said, "it's a free country and I've got a passport. I'll get there on my own."

"I guess there's no way of stopping a Cherokee on the warpath."

They stared at each other across what seemed to Dusty to be an emotional chasm as deep and as wide as the Grand Canyon. She felt lost and lonely.

Mack muttered something to himself and he moved from the table in her direction. Dusty rose from her chair. Her knees felt weak. They were only inches apart. For a heart-stopping moment, seeing the raging emotions in Mack's eyes, she thought he was going to crush her in his arms and kiss her.

Instead, he turned and stalked out of the room, slamming the door after him.

Chapter Twelve

That night, Dusty had a telephone call from Nevada.

"Dusty!" a familiar male voice said. "I miss you out here. When are you coming back?"

She smiled at the sound of Grant Packer's deep voice. "Hi, Grant. I'm glad you called."

"You sound depressed."

"I am, sort of. That's why I'm glad you called. Cheer me up."

"I could do a better job of that if you were out here. I repeat: when are you coming back?"

"Not for a while, I'm afraid. Looks like I'll be headed for South America."

"South America! Why the hell do you want to go down there?"

"Business. That's where the story is breaking."

"Oh, yeah, that kidnapping thing. Wish you could have passed that one up and stayed with me. Will you be coming back to me as soon as it's over?"

"I—I'm not sure right now, Grant. I have some decisions to make."

There was a brief silence. Then Grant said in a softer voice, "You know how I feel about you, Dusty. We haven't known each other very long, but I've come to care a lot for you. Things have been very dull around here since you left."

Dusty smiled. She had been in a black mood ever since seeing Mack. Talking to Grant cheered her up.

"How's the film going?" she asked.

"As well as can be expected at this point. We're on schedule, which is good. We're running over budget, which is bad. All par for the course."

She laughed. "Have you been in any more fight scenes?"

"Yeah. Just about got my lights punched out yesterday. That stuntman forgot we were making a movie and waded into me. He was knocking me all over the ring. I finally got mad and flattened him. Took half a dozen from the camera crew to get us separated. No hard feelings, though. He and I got drunk together last night."

Dusty grinned. "Wish I could have seen that fight."

"Wish you could have, too. Dusty, have you made a decision about doing that book with me? You know how much I want your help."

Just the book? she thought. "No, Grant, I haven't made a decision. I need some time to think it over. That's why I took this assignment. Maybe I'll have an answer for you when I get back from South America.''

''I might start missing you so much I'll fly down there to see you.''

''You have a picture to make, remember?''

After talking with Grant, Dusty called Myra to brief her on her progress. ''I'm starting to get some breaks in this story.''

''Terrific. What's developed?''

Dusty thought about the story she could do: ''Corporation Executive Plans Commando Raid to Free Kidnap Victim.'' It would make one hell of a story—if she could print it. She sighed. ''I can't give you any details yet, Myra. But I'm going to fly to South America. All I can tell you is that I might get an exclusive on the showdown with the kidnappers.''

''That sounds fantastic. When are you leaving?''

''Tomorrow or the next day, I think. I'll be in touch with you from down there.''

''Okay.''

''Myra...keep all this under wraps for now. I don't want other reporters to find out why I'm going there, or they'll suspect I've stumbled on some inside info and that would blow the whole thing. There's a lot of the media down there now with all the civil strife. I'll pretend to cover the pending revolution.''

''All right—mum's the word.''

Dusty had a tough time booking a flight to the capital city. Just as Bob Nicholson had warned, flights were erratic and uncertain. She spent an entire day in the Dallas airport before she finally got onto a flight.

She saw several other reporters on the plane, and a number of nationals returning home.

The capital of the South American country was a picturesque city surrounded by hills rising to the towering Andes. Parrots in bright red, green and yellow plumage fluttered in the branches of the tropical jungle. Great falls cascaded from towering cliffs into pools of icy-clear water from which black panthers drank. In places, the jungle had been cleared for coffee and banana plantations.

The air in the city had the crisp coolness of the high altitude even though it was the middle of the South American summer. Along the broad main thoroughfare were modern office buildings constructed of concrete, glass and chrome in stark contrast to the jungle only a few miles away. It was a beautiful city that until recently had been a tourist attraction. Now buildings were sandbagged, there were barbed-wire barricades on street corners and tanks rumbled down the main avenue.

When Dusty landed at the airport she took a cab to her hotel. The cab was a battered twenty-year-old yellow Ford that left a plume of smoke behind it as it spun out of the airport with a screech. The driver was a swarthy young man in his early twenties who wore a T-shirt with the name of an American rock band stamped on it. He turned and flashed Dusty a friendly smile. "You American, lady?"

"That's right."

"Pleased to meet you. My name, Julio. I speak real good English."

"Yes, you do."

"I learn super good English listening to American radio and music. I'm going to America one day and get rich."

Dusty suppressed a smile. "You think all Americans are rich?"

"Sure. You a newspaper lady?"

"Yes."

"Anything you want to know, you ask Julio. I take you anywhere you want to go. Lots of people down here don't like Americans. You don't trust anybody. But you can trust Julio. I like Americans. I gonna be one someday. You let Julio take you around. This dangerous place now. You want something on black market? Julio get it for you."

They had arrived at one of the buildings on the main avenue—a modern hotel.

Julio hopped out and grabbed her suitcase. "You want to go someplace, you look for Julio's cab. I hang around here a lot. This is where rich Americans stay."

"All right, Julio. Thanks." She paid the cab fare and tipped him for carrying her bag into the hotel. The lobby was filled with media people who had come to cover the political turmoil firsthand.

If her instincts were right, Bob Nicholson's commando group would begin arriving before the week was out.

While she waited for the little private army to arrive, Dusty decided to join the other reporters covering the street demonstrations. After unpacking in her room, she slung her camera case over her shoulder and went downstairs. When she stepped outside, she saw a familiar battered yellow Ford. Julio opened a door and ran up to her. "You ready to see the town? Julio take you. Best guide in town."

She couldn't keep from laughing at the young man's persistent salesmanship. "All right, Julio."

The smoking old cab took them through the wide main streets and down narrow side streets. Dusty had Julio stop often while she snapped pictures of mobs marching down streets shouting slogans and waving banners in support of "El Hombre." She caught shots of clashes with club-wielding police and soldiers, of water cannons and canisters spewing tear gas.

"Just like Iran and Beirut," she muttered.

On the third day she had breakfast, then wandered into the spacious lobby where she settled onto a couch with a portable lap computer to make notes.

She had become absorbed in the story when a familiar voice interrupted her. "Think you'll find any woodpeckers down here?"

She glanced up, not at all surprised to see Mack. He pulled up a chair beside hers and sat in it. He was giving her a smoldering look.

"Yes, I think I'll find about a half-dozen woodpeckers," she said calmly, meeting his eyes with a level gaze. "As a matter of fact, I have just spotted one of them."

"You're really something, you know that?" Mack said in an exasperated tone, keeping his voice low. "How did you know we'd be coming here?"

"Elementary, my dear Watson," she quipped. "Those maps all over the walls in Nicholson's ranch house—they all had this area circled. See? You might as well have let me come with you."

Mack crossed his arms, looking at her thoughtfully. "I was hoping you wouldn't be able to locate our base of operations, but I should have known better. I might have known you'd track us down. You can be a pain in the neck sometimes, Dusty, but I have to admit you're good at your job."

"Is the rest of your group here? You might as well tell me. I'll find out."

He nodded. "You probably will. No, they're not here yet, but they'll be arriving later today or tomorrow."

"Well, now that I know all about it, are you going to let me in on all your plans?"

His look hardened. "Dusty, if you do something to screw up this operation—"

"Just what do you think I'd do, Mack O'Shea?" she asked angrily.

"I'm not sure. You'd do anything for a good story. I don't want to see you taking pictures of our people. To be on the safe side, leave your camera in your room."

"Don't be ridiculous. Reporters are running all over town taking pictures."

"And don't call me 'Mack' if we're around other people. My name is Martin Smith. I'm a contractor from Dayton, Ohio, here to inspect the Nicholson oil field operation."

"Oh-ho. Forged passport, huh? I guess an ex-CIA agent would know people who do that sort of thing. Couldn't you think of a more original name than Smith?"

"It's easy to remember. Do you want to go for a ride?"

Dusty looked at him with surprise. "Ever since you found me at the Nicholson ranch, you've been treating me like a communicable disease. Why do you want me to go riding with you? So you can lose me in the jungle?"

"That's a thought. But, no, I've become resigned. As the old saying goes, 'If you can't lick 'em, you might as well join 'em.' Obviously, you're going to be sticking your nose in everything we do, so it might be better if I have you around where I can keep an eye on you. Besides, nothing is going to happen until the rest of the group gets here, so we might as well do some sight-seeing. I have a rented car."

"That's not a very gracious invitation. I'm not sure I want to go sight-seeing with you."

He shrugged and rose from his chair. "Suit yourself."

She put her computer in her briefcase. "Don't go getting huffy. I'd love to go for a ride."

In Mack's rented car, they drove out of the hotel garage and headed down the main thoroughfare.

A battered yellow Ford pulled away from the street in front of the hotel at the same time.

Mack glanced in his rearview mirror several times. "I think we're being followed."

Dusty turned and looked behind them. "That's Julio's cab."

"Julio?"

"He's appointed himself my personal guide ever since he brought me from the airport."

"Why is he following us?"

"Search me. Julio is a very ambitious young man. He has plans to become rich. Maybe he's trying to get a lead on where we're headed. He seems to know everything that's going on in the city, or at least he likes to give that impression.''

''Well, I think we've lost him.''

Mack fell silent, concentrating on driving carefully around the sandbagged machine-gun emplacements and barbed-wire barricades in the main streets. They were stopped several times by armed soldiers checking their papers.

Dusty wondered at her own emotions as she sat next to the man she had loved enough to marry, the man with whom she had shared the most intimate moments of her life, and who was now a stranger. She felt pain and sadness at the rift that had come between them, a rift that seemed beyond repair.

How did Mack feel about her? He had not given the slightest indication that he had changed his mind about anything. He had not even mentioned her wedding ring, which she had pinned on the pillow. Judging from the cold way he was acting toward her, he must consider their marriage to be over.

Yet when he looked at her, she could see powerful emotions churning in his eyes, emotions that equalled hers. But whatever he was feeling, he was keeping it to himself.

His remarks about her and Grant Packer had been cutting, implying that he believed she was carrying on an affair with Packer. That's probably why he was so cold and distant now, she thought. He was mad enough at her leaving her wedding ring in Monterrey. Added to that was her going on to California to do the Packer interview instead of agreeing to give up her career and settle down with him in Dallas. Now, piled on all that was bitterness that she could possibly be involved with another man so soon after leaving him.

Her thoughts were interrupted.

"That's where the president lives," Mack said, nodding toward an imposing mansion surrounded by a wall. Armed soldiers were stationed at all the entrances.

"Looks more like a fortress," Dusty observed.

"By our standards, he's more of a dictator than a president. He's been in office for ten years. They have elections down here, but they're usually rigged. There's a strong revolutionary movement gaining momentum. We think the kidnappers are in the political camp with the underground revolutionary party and they have friends in political prisons. They all hate Americans because they think we've been supporting the present government, so they'd think nothing of murdering Emory Wilson if they don't get what they want."

Farther on, they passed the city's opera building. In contrast to the ultramodern architecture of the office buildings on the main thoroughfare, the opera house was an ornate Gothic structure, resembling something from the Middle Ages. It, too, was surrounded by sandbags and barbed wire and guarded by soldiers.

Away from the center of town were open markets where sides of beef hung in the open air along with bins of vegetables and fruits. In another part of the *marcado* were garments, leather goods, jewelry and crafts of all descriptions.

Still farther from the heart of the city were the slums, endless blocks of shacks and hovels that housed the urban poor.

"I can see why there's political unrest," Dusty murmured.

"Coffee and bananas have been the chief source of the country's revenue," Mack said, "but recently, oil began playing a part in the economy. Several American oil companies have drilled here, including Nicholson. *El presidente* doesn't have a lot of use for North Americans, but he's tolerated the American oil companies because he desperately needs the money from the oil fields. The country's deeply in hock to international banks and about to default on its loans. Now I'll show you the Nicholson operation."

He took a road to the south that cut through the jungle away from the city. Dusty was surprised to find that it was paved.

"The Nicholson Corporation paid for having the road built," Mack explained. "We needed it to transport machinery to the oil fields."

Presently the jungle gave way to some open plains and they came to a fence with a sign over the gate, Nicholson Oil Company.

"Emory Wilson was kidnapped on this spot," Mack told Dusty. "He was leaving the plant office out here late one afternoon. He drove through this gate and was stopped by men in a van. Some workers inside the fence saw the men drag Wilson out of his car and put him in the van. Then the van sped off. It all happened too fast for anybody to try to stop them. All we have to go on is a description of the vehicle: a battered old blue American-made van."

"Look," Dusty said, "there are soldiers stationed at the gates."

"Yeah. We think the government is about to nationalize all foreign-owned interests, including the oil-field operations. We're shutting down the offices here and moving all personnel back to the States."

Mack showed some papers to a guard now stationed at the gate and he waved them on. The road took them past some drilling sites to a cluster of tin-roofed buildings. Near one of the buildings was a heliport. A helicopter with Nicholson Oil painted on one side was next to it.

Mack stared at it silently.

"Are you planning to use that helicopter in the rescue operation?" Dusty asked.

"If we can get to it," Mack replied succinctly.

"I guess you know what the government would do to you guys if they find out what you're up to."

"I don't think they'd be too happy."

"They'd put you so far back in jail they'd have to feed you with a slingshot."

"That's possible."

She could see Mack had fallen into one of his uncommunicative moods, so she made no further attempt at conversation.

They entered the city limits, passing again through the slum area. Mack broke the silence. "Hungry?"

She nodded. "Yes, now that you mention it."

"Let's see what the *marcado* has to offer."

In the market they found a sidewalk restaurant where they bought tropical fruits, fresh bread, cheese and wine. Then they wandered between the stalls of the vendors. When Dusty exclaimed with delight over a handmade silver bracelet, each link embossed with an Inca design, Mack said he would buy it for her. She tried to protest, but he insisted and handed the vendor several bills of South American currency.

Dusty felt a sudden suffusion of soft warmth. Her eyes blurred tearfully as she slipped the bracelet on her wrist. For the first time since they had parted in Monterrey, the anger and bitterness that had been such a wall between them seemed less formidable. When she looked at Mack, his rugged features were softened by her haze of tears. She was flooded with a sudden rush of poignant memories . . . all the good times they had shared . . . the laughs . . . the adventures . . . the love-making . . .

They said very little on the way back to the hotel. Dusty wondered if Mack was experiencing the same emotions. She began to feel a tiny glimmer of hope for them.

Why would Mack have spent the morning with her unless he still cared for her?

She dared to fantasize that they would find a way to patch up their differences. They would have a long talk. Somehow, she would convince Mack that there was nothing between her and Grant Packer. In turn, he would tell her that he realized how important her career was to her and that things were going to be like they used to be. He would stop trying to rearrange her life to suit his plans. Then he would take her in his arms and there would be kisses and a passionate reunion. . . .

She was lost in the fantasy when they walked into the hotel lobby. A tall, attractive blond woman rose from a lobby sofa and walked toward them. Dusty was so involved with her dreamy state that she was only half aware of her surroundings.

Vaguely, she heard the woman say, "Hi, I've been wondering where you'd gone. I've been nervous here with all the soldiers around."

She slipped her arm through Mack's, smiling up at him, then gave Dusty a curious look.

The fantasy fell around Dusty like shattered glass. She stared at the woman.

"We took a drive out to the plant to check on the helicopter," Mack explained. "Laura, I don't think you've ever met Dusty. Dusty, this is Laura Nicholson."

Dusty felt as if her body had turned to stone as she stared at Mack's former fiancée.

"Hello," Laura said with a cool smile.

Dusty stammered, "I—I didn't know you were here."

"Yes." She smiled up at Mack again. "Mack and I arrived yesterday."

The words slammed into Dusty with stunning blows. All the warmth she had felt moments before turned to bitter ashes. She went cold with fury remembering her conversation with Mack back at the Nicholson ranch. She'd asked, "When do we leave for South America?" and Mack had replied, "I'm leaving in a few days. You're not going anywhere."

He had refused to let her accompany him. Yet he had flown down here with Bob Nicholson's daughter. They had checked into the hotel together. Were they sharing the same room?

"Excuse me," she said. She walked away from them, barely able to see the elevator through burning tears.

In her room, she ripped off the bracelet Mack had bought her and flung it away from her. Then she fell on the bed and sobbed.

She stayed in her room the rest of the afternoon. She was so miserable, she had half a mind to chuck the whole assignment and take the first plane back to the States. Why let herself in for any more pain? She could do the book with Grant Packer. He was an exciting, attractive man who flattered her with his attention. He could offer her the kind of travel and adventure she liked.

When it was time for dinner she went down to the hotel restaurant and sat in a corner booth, hoping to avoid any encounter with Mack or Laura Nicholson. She sipped her drink but only picked at the meal. Then she went back to her room.

She had been back only a few minutes when there was a soft tap at her door. She opened it. Laura Nicholson stood in the doorway. "May I come in?"

Numbly, Dusty moved aside. Laura entered the room. Dusty closed the door before turning to face the blonde. So this was the other woman in Mack O'Shea's life, she thought. Laura was smartly dressed in a designer frock. Her thick blond hair was pulled back in a bun. She looked cool, poised and fashionable.

Why shouldn't she? Dusty thought bitterly. Laura Nicholson had not grown up in a little Oklahoma crossroads town where her father ran a general store and filling station. Laura Nicholson had attended finishing schools. Her clothes were from Neiman-Marcus. The self-assurance of a wealthy background surrounded her like a golden aura. She was a beautiful woman. Why shouldn't Mack find her attractive? More than that, she was quite ready to settle down and make Mack the kind of wife he wanted. How could Dusty compete?

"I thought perhaps we should talk," Laura said.

Dusty shrugged. "What do we have to talk about?"

"How about Mack O'Shea, for starters?"

Dusty felt her blood boil. "I don't think that's a very pleasant subject."

Laura's voice was soft. "But it's one we can't avoid. May I sit down?"

"Help yourself."

Laura sat on the side of the bed as Dusty uneasily settled herself into a nearby chair.

Laura was silent for a moment as if gathering her thoughts. "I don't mind telling you frankly, Dusty, that although we never met before this, I hated you for coming between Mack and me. We'd known each other since college. I'd planned my whole life around him. Our wedding was all arranged, everything set. Then . . . just weeks before the ceremony, Mack came home from an assignment to the mideast.

"Something about him had changed. I sensed it immediately. At first he wouldn't admit it . . . then he finally told me that he'd met a woman when he was in Beirut; you, of course. He broke our engagement, flew to New York . . . and the next thing I knew he'd married you."

"I'm sorry," Dusty said. "I know how upset you must have been. But I didn't deliberately take Mack away from you and he wasn't treating you cruelly. He agonized over the situation. He finally decided that he'd be even more unfair to marry you when he was in love with somebody else." Then Dusty added heavily, "Anyway, that's ancient history now."

"Yes, I know," Laura said slowly. "You're separated. I have a second chance."

"Looks like you're making the most of it," Dusty muttered. "Congratulations."

"I'm not sure congratulations are in order yet, though I have hopes. Mack has talked with me about the problems you've had. Now that I've met you, I can see why he became infatuated with you, Dusty. You have an unusual, wild, elusive beauty. Apparently most men find you attractive. I've been reading about your involvement with Grant Packer."

"Don't believe everything you read," Dusty said.

"No? I'm inclined to go along with the old saying, 'Where there's smoke there's fire.' But that's beside the point. As I was saying, I can see why Mack found you so desirable. But there has to be more to it than that to make a solid marriage. Mack wants to settle down. He wants stability in his life, his marriage, his family. He wants a normal home life. Your career takes you on assignments all over the world . . . often dangerous assignments. I can be the kind of wife Mack wants, Dusty. I'd be very good for Mack, for his future, his career."

"Then what's the problem?" Dusty asked bitterly. "You seem to have the inside track. He came down here with you, not with me."

"Yes, he did, didn't he?"

"Why did you come down here?" Dusty asked. "This isn't exactly the safest place in the world to be right now."

"I know. Daddy raised a big fuss. But I wanted to be with Mack." She gazed at Dusty thoughtfully. "I want to be sure you and Mack are through, that you aren't going to continue popping in and out of his life."

"Maybe you should be talking to him."

"Oh, I have . . . and we've reached—well, an understanding. Mack tells me you've already filed for divorce. He won't contest it."

Dusty found the conversation increasingly painful. "Why are you telling me all this?"

"Because I hope you'll come to realize that the best thing you can do for Mack is to stay out of his life. You had your chance, and you can't make him happy. The two of you are simply incompatible."

Dusty rose, moved to the window and looked out, hiding her tears.

Laura went on, "Mack and I have the basis for a good, solid marriage. You'll do yourself and everyone involved a favor if you'll quietly bow out of his life now. Mack realizes he made a mistake when he broke our engagement to marry you. He was infatuated with you, but it's me he really loves."

Dusty blinked back the scalding tears. "You could have saved yourself the trouble of coming here," she said numbly. "I already made up my mind that things between Mack and me are hopeless. I won't hang around much longer. As soon as I finish this assignment, I'm flying back to the States."

She heard the bed rustle as Laura rose. "You're very sensible, Dusty," Laura said softly. "I don't want us to be enemies. If I can help you with your story I'll be more than glad to do so. Daddy is flying in tomorrow. He's very grateful to you for not making his plans public. He respects you for that and I'm sure he'll cooperate with you and keep you posted on any developments."

Dusty nodded.

Laura moved up behind her and gave her arm a squeeze. Then she left.

Dusty thought it might have been easier if she could hate Laura Nicholson, but there didn't seem much point in it. As much as it hurt, she thought Laura was right. She and Mack were incompatible. Laura could no doubt be the kind of wife Mack needed.

Chapter Thirteen

Dusty rose early the following morning. As if joining in her dismal mood, the sky turned dark and a tropical storm swept across the city. Dusty donned a raincoat and, carrying an umbrella, went outside. For once, Julio's cab was nowhere in sight. Maybe, she thought, it wouldn't start in the rain.

She sloshed along the sidewalks as the rain drummed on her umbrella. She felt a compulsion to keep moving. She was afraid that if she sat in her lonely hotel room, staring out at the sheets of rain, she'd go bananas.

"I wish I'd never met you, Mack O'Shea," she whispered, her tears mingling with the raindrops. "I didn't know anything could hurt this much...."

It was late in the afternoon when she finally returned to the hotel, weary and sore. She stopped at the desk to check for messages and was handed a note. "Have been trying to reach you. Please call me in room 231. Bob Nicholson."

So, she thought, the president of the Nicholson Corporation had arrived.

Dusty took the elevator to her floor. In her room she shed her raincoat and called room 231. The deep, cultured voice of Bob Nicholson answered.

"Mr. Nicholson, this is Dusty O'Shea."

"Oh, yes, Mrs. O'Shea. I've called your room several times. There are some things I'd like to discuss with you as soon as it's convenient."

"Any time is fine with me, as soon as I get into some dry clothes. I've been out in the rain."

"Yes, it's coming down in torrents, isn't it? How does an early dinner in the hotel dining room strike you?"

"All right. Give me a half hour."

"I'll meet you in the cocktail lounge downstairs."

Dusty stripped off her damp jeans and stepped into a hot shower. Why did the president of the Nicholson Corporation want to have dinner with her? What was so important that he wanted to talk to her about? Did it have something to do with the kidnapping? Or did he want to talk to her about Laura and Mack? She hoped not. She'd had about all of that subject she could take.

After the shower, she brushed her hair, repaired her makeup and put on the one acceptable dress she had brought on the trip. She took the elevator downstairs and found the tall, distinguished oil-company executive waiting in the cocktail lounge. He smiled in recognition when she entered the room, and rose to greet her.

"I think we can talk more comfortably in the dining room, Mrs. O'Shea. I have a table reserved."

He escorted her into the dining room, where the hostess seated them at a table in an isolated corner of the room. They were beside a window. Night had fallen but the rain was still coming down, splashing against the window. In the glass, Dusty could see their reflection, the tall man with silver hair seated across from her, the flickering candle on the table between them.

"Hope you don't mind all this security business," Nicholson apologized in a low voice, "but we have to be careful. I don't want to tip our hand to either the government's secret police or the kidnappers. It's quite possible my room could be bugged. I think it's safe to talk here."

Dusty nodded. "I understand."

"I have several things I wanted to discuss with you, Mrs. O'Shea. First, I haven't had a chance to thank you personally for keeping our plans from the media. I want you to know that I am very grateful. Not all reporters would show that much character and sense of responsibility. They sometimes disregard the victims if it means a big story. You could have ruined all our plans but you didn't. You've earned my confidence and respect."

"I didn't see how I could do otherwise under the circumstances," Dusty replied, "though I still hope to get a story out of this."

"Of course, and I told you that if you'd cooperate with us, I'd do the same for you. You played fair with me and I'll play fair with you. I'm not one to forget a favor. Now...there have been some important developments. All of our people are in the country now, under various names and identities. I'm the only one who came in openly using my own name. As president of the Nicholson Corporation, there is nothing unusual in my flying down here from time to time to personally check on our company operation. I receive a certain amount of respect from the local authorities and the government officials because this country needs our oil. But I have to be extremely careful not to let anyone associate me with our rescue operation."

He stopped talking abruptly as a waiter approached the table. Nicholson gave him their order for dinner.

After the waiter left, Dusty prompted, "You say there have been some new developments?"

"Yes. We've had more communication from the kidnappers. They have upped the price for Emory's release to five million dollars."

"Are you going to pay it?"

"Yes, of course we would to save Emory's life. Unfortunately, the other strings are still attached—the release of the political prisoners. I am going to the U.S. embassy in the morning and to the head of the police department. I don't know if it will do any good, but I've got to try. I thought you might like to go with me."

Dusty's pulse quickened. "Yes, indeed I would."

"You're welcome to ride to the meeting with me, but again I have to trust you to keep quiet until we have Emory and everyone involved in the rescue operation safely out of the country. Then you can break the story. You'll have an exclusive scoop. Now, do I have your word again to keep all this off the record until it's over?''

The excitement temporarily helped to dull her personal misery. ''I appreciate your letting me in on this, Mr. Nicholson. And, yes, you have my word.''

He smiled. ''Good. Now let's enjoy the dinner.''

Their first call the next morning was to the U.S. embassy. The meeting was brief and fruitless. The embassy personnel were scurrying around cleaning out desks and shredding papers.

Nicholson was able to have a short meeting with an embassy official. ''I'm sorry, Bob,'' he said. ''There's damn little we can do to help at this point. It's only a matter of days, maybe hours before this whole country erupts like a volcano. There are air-force transport planes waiting at the airport to ferry my people home. We have orders to shut down except for the barest skeleton staff. We have to be out of here by tonight. Believe me, I wish there was more we could do, but this whole thing is in the hands of the local police and military now.''

From the embassy, they drove to police headquarters and talked with the detective in charge of the kidnapping case. He was a small, dark man with a scrubby beard. He looked harassed and tired. His suit was rumpled. His eyes were red-rimmed.

In precise English, he said, ''We are doing what we can, Mr. Nicholson. There are very few leads. Nobody got the license plate of the vehicle in which your vice president was kidnapped. The description given by the workers could fit any male over twenty-one in this country. I could give you a list of the revolutionary fanatics that would reach around this building and any one of them could be a suspect.''

Bob Nicholson glared at the detective as he pounded the desk with his fist. ''An innocent man's life is hanging by a thread! They've threatened to kill Emory in a few days unless their demands are made. I'm ready to pay the ransom. Will you release their prisoners?''

''I can't do that! And it wouldn't do any good. They'd take your money and when the prisoners were released, they'd shoot your vice president anyway. That's the way these terrorists operate.'' He made a helpless gesture. ''I'm sorry, Mr. Nicholson, but right now people are getting killed all over the city. The government cares very little about one American, and the revolutionaries even less. I care because the law is my profession, but I just don't have any new leads.''

When they left the building, it looked to Dusty as if Bob Nicholson had aged ten years. ''I keep thinking about Emory's wife and children,'' he muttered. ''If something happens to him, I'll never forgive myself. I feel so damn impotent!'' He slammed his fist into his palm.

They got in his rented car and started back to the hotel. When they turned a corner, they were suddenly confronted by a shouting, angry mob that filled the street from curb to curb. The signs they carried bore the ubiquitous drawings of El Hombre. A rock flew through the air and smashed one of the car windows. Dusty felt icy fingers clamp her stomach. The crowd suddenly converged on the car, shaking their fists, shouting curses and hurling rocks.

Nicholson tried to back up, but the car was surrounded. The crowd was pounding the windows with their fists. Dusty gasped as a face, distorted with rage, pressed against her window. She went numb with terror.

"My God!" Nicholson choked, his face pale. It was more of a prayer than an exclamation. "Why are they attacking us?"

Suddenly there was an added commotion. A car was forcing its way through the crowd, its horn blaring. Dusty jerked around. She saw a battered yellow Ford, smoke pouring from its tail pipe. Hysterical laughter bubbled up in her throat.

Julio's taxi forced its way next to Nicholson's car. Julio rolled his window down and started shouting at the crowd, waving his fist at them. They shouted back.

Dusty couldn't make out what was said, but whatever Julio had said seemed to have an effect. Some of the crowd drew back enough for Julio to open his door. He motioned frantically to Dusty.

"Come on!" she cried to Bob Nicholson. "This man is a friend."

She got her door open, scrambled out and into the back seat of Julio's cab. Nicholson piled in behind her. Julio slammed and locked their door, then hopped behind the wheel. Blaring his horn, yelling at the crowd and making obscene gestures, he tried to drive forward. Just then there was the sound of helicopter blades beating the air above them. Canisters crashed to the ground, spewing great plumes of acrid smoke.

"Tear gas!" Nicholson exclaimed.

The crowd, gasping and choking, scattered in all directions. The street cleared in less than a minute.

Julio drove as fast as his rattling, smoking old car would travel.

After a somewhat delayed reaction, Dusty began shivering violently. She gritted her teeth, trying to keep them from chattering.

When they were several blocks away, Julio pulled over, turned and grinned at them. "Very bad, you go driving around by yourself. You should get Julio to take you, like I said. City very bad now. People angry."

"Yes, thank you, Julio," Dusty said with heartfelt emotion. "I was scared out of my wits. How did you find us?"

"I follow. Figure you get in trouble. Hello, mister, my name Julio." He reached across the seat to shake Bob Nicholson's hand.

"My name is Bob Nicholson, Julio. I join in thanking you. I don't mind telling you I was scared, too. No telling what might have happened to us."

"Oh, you Mr. Nicholson, the rich American with the oil wells." Julio nodded wisely. "I know. I try to get job at your oil company. No luck."

"Well, I'd see that you had a job there now, but unfortunately it looks as if the government is taking over our operation."

"Maybe you take me to the U.S.? Give me a job in your company there?"

Nicholson smiled. "I'd be glad to give you the job, but I'm not sure getting you into the U.S. would be so simple."

"I read about you in paper. One of your people kidnapped, *sí*? The terrorists take him. Very bad."

"Yes, it's very bad."

Julio shook his head, frowning thoughtfully. "You know where they take him?"

"No. We just came from police headquarters. They can't seem to help."

"The police!" Julio snorted disdainfully. "They know nothing. I find out for you."

Nicholson smiled. "I wish you could, Julio."

"There be a reward, maybe?"

"Of course. A big reward."

"How big?"

"Julio, I'd give anybody five hundred thousand dollars for a lead to where the kidnappers are holding Emory Wilson."

Julio whistled softly. "American dollars?"

"Yes."

Julio's eyes had become bright with excitement. "I take you back to hotel. You stay where it's safe. Julio find out. I come tonight."

He turned around and started off with a screech of tires that threw Bob Nicholson and Dusty back against the seat.

After Julio had dropped them off at the hotel, Nicholson chuckled. "I don't know if we were safer with the mob or with Julio. You don't think he could actually turn up some lead to the kidnappers' hideout, do you?"

"I wouldn't sell Julio short," Dusty said. "He seems to know just about everything that's going on in this city. He's certainly streetwise."

"Well, at this point I'm grasping at straws. Mack is out trying to make contact with people he knows in the CIA who might have some leads. Maybe something will turn up." Then he said, "After that harrowing experience, I could use a strong drink. Can I buy you one?''

''Best offer I've had all day.''

That night, the phone in Dusty's room rang. When she picked it up, the desk clerk told her a man downstairs wanted to meet her in the lobby. ''Said to tell you his name is Julio.''

''I'll be right down.''

Julio was standing near the entrance. He motioned to Dusty with his head and went out to his cab. Dusty followed, getting into the back seat.

Julio started the cab and slowly drove away from the hotel. He looked straight ahead as he said, ''Have to be very careful. Many eyes watching. Best to talk in taxi.''

''What do you want to talk to me about?''

''Julio find out what you want to know.''

For a moment Dusty was speechless. ''You know where the kidnappers are holding Emory Wilson?''

''The American businessman. Yes, I know. You tell Mr. Nicholson. I come back to hotel in an hour. I take you to place we can talk.''

Julio circled several blocks, then returned to the hotel. ''One hour,'' he said, as Dusty left the cab.

She hurried to her room and immediately called Nicholson's suite. ''I have to see you right away,'' she said when he answered the phone.

''All right. Will the bar do?''

''Yes, but we have to be careful.''

In the cocktail lounge, Nicholson ordered martinis. They sat at the most secluded table. Dusty bent over her drink. In a low voice, she said, ''Julio contacted me. He's coming back in an hour. He wants us to go with him. He says he has information about where the kidnappers are holding Emory Wilson."

Nicholson stared at her. His hands holding the thin-stemmed glass trembled. "Can you believe him?"

"I don't know. It's worth a try."

"We could be walking into some kind of trap. I want Colonel Sawyer along. Let's go up and have a conference with him."

"I don't like it," Sawyer growled when they broke the news to him in his room. "A street kid. A taxi driver. What do you know about him? He could be in cahoots with the kidnappers. They could be planning to nab you, Bob. What a prize you'd make! The head of the Nicholson Corporation, one of the richest men in America!"

"What do you propose we do? I can't just ignore this. There's an outside chance he's onto something."

"All right, we'll check it out. But you stay here."

Promptly on time, Julio's ancient car pulled up in front of the hotel in a cloud of smoke. Dusty, accompanied by Colonel Sawyer, hurried out to the cab.

Julio frowned at Sawyer.

"It's all right, Julio," Dusty said. "Mr. Nicholson couldn't come, so he sent his close, trusted associate. This is Colonel Sawyer."

"Okay." Julio nodded. "Is all right, you say so, lady."

He pulled out into the darkened streets and started on a drive that took them through what seemed an endless maze of back streets. Several times they were stopped by soldiers because they were violating the curfew laws now in effect, but Julio said something to them in a low voice that apparently satisfied them and they waved him on.

At last they stopped in front of a small adobe café on a narrow, dark street. "My Uncle Arturo's *cantina*," Julio explained.

He hurried around and opened the door for them and they all went inside. The place had a dirt floor. A few battered and scarred tables and chairs were the only furnishings beside a rough bar. Kerosene lamps supplied dim lighting.

A fat man came from behind the bar, wiping his hand on his apron. "My Uncle Arturo," Julio introduced. In rapid Spanish, he told the saloon keeper that these were his friends and he wished to buy them a round of drinks. His overweight relative nodded, went to the bar and presently returned with drinks that were placed before each of them.

"This, you must drink slowly," Julio warned. "Much strong."

Dusty took a sip and gasped. "I see what you mean," she said when she got her breath back.

She could tell by the dark scowl on Colonel Sawyer's face that he was growing impatient. "We didn't come here to sample your uncle's liquor. You say you have information for us?"

"Yes. You wait one minute. This man come."

Dusty tried another sip of the drink and her head started swimming. She hated to think what condition she'd be in if she emptied the glass.

A tall, slender man wearing a wide-brimmed slouch hat entered the *cantina*. He stood at the bar for a moment, talking to Arturo in a low voice. Then he turned and exchanged looks with Julio, who nodded to him.

"This is the man we come to see," Julio explained.

The man moved to their table. His hat was pulled low over his forehead, casting dark shadows over the upper portion of his face. In the dim, flickering light from the lamps, Dusty could only see his mouth and unshaven jaw. He had brought a drink with him from the bar. He held it with long, nervous fingers. He spoke to Julio in such a low voice that Dusty could not make out the words.

Julio said, "He wants money for what he can tell you."

Sawyer grunted. "How much?"

"A thousand dollars, American money."

The gruff old military man snorted. "I give him a thousand dollars for what? A fairy story! How do I know he's telling the truth?"

Julio and the man again spoke in low tones in an exchange that grew heated. Finally, in a disdainful gesture, the man tossed something on the table. Sawyer picked it up. He frowned, then swore softly under his breath. He handed it to Dusty. She saw that it was a Polaroid snapshot. It was very poor quality, but there was no question—from news stories she'd seen, she recognized Emory Wilson. He was seated on a rough bench in a small, bare room. His hands were tied behind his back.

From a pocket, Sawyer drew a roll of American bills. He counted off a thousand dollars and laid it on the table. The man's long, nervous fingers moved like a quick, long-legged spider, scooping it up and jamming it in a pocket. He downed his drink in a swallow, and wiped the back of his hand across his mouth.

Then he produced a crudely drawn map. He jabbed a finger at a spot that had been circled.

A moment later, he was gone.

"Come," Julio said, rising. "We go. Not good to stay here too long."

In the cab on the way back to the hotel, Colonel Sawyer said, "You seem to know your way around the streets, Julio."

"You bet. You want to know, you ask Julio."

"How are you with the black market?"

"Anything you want, Julio get."

"What if I asked you to get things that the government doesn't allow?"

Julio made a derisive sound. "The soldiers only allow what you can't pay for. You got enough money, you get anything."

"How about guns?" Sawyer asked cautiously.

"Sure. What you want? Shotguns? Automatics? Grenades? You got the money, then Julio get what you want."

"All right. I want you to come to the hotel early tomorrow morning. I'll have the money. But I need guns and ammunition by tomorrow night. You think you can get it by then?"

"Sure. Can do it."

Dusty leaned forward with a worried frown. "Julio, don't get yourself hurt doing this."

Julio laughed. "Nothing hurt Julio...too smart."

He pulled up at the hotel.

Late the following day, Bob Nicholson called Dusty to tell her they were holding a council of war that night and she was welcome to ride with him.

At the appointed time, she went downstairs and through the lobby to the parking garage. Bob Nicholson was waiting beside another car he had rented. Without a word, he opened the door for her, got behind the wheel and pulled out into the street.

The rain was still falling in a heavy downpour. The windshield wipers moved in an arc with a steady clicking sound. Nicholson spoke very little as they drove. Dusty saw in his face that the strain was beginning to tell on him. When he took a hand from the wheel to rub his chin, she saw that his hand was trembling.

She realized they had taken the road that led to the Nicholson Corporation plant. When they passed through the gate, the two soldiers stationed there merely glanced at them, then looked away.

"Colonel Sawyer was out here earlier and bribed the sentries," Nicholson explained. "They won't give us any trouble."

The metal-roofed buildings at the Nicholson drilling site looked dark and deserted. They drove around, sloshing through mud puddles, finally stopping at a small building near the warehouse where two other rented cars were parked. Lined up beside them were three Jeeps.

Dusty put on her trench coat, adjusted the hood and ducked out into the rain. She followed Nicholson, who hurried in long strides to the building. He unlocked the door with a key, motioned her inside, then closed and locked the door behind them.

Inside, Dusty saw that the lights were on but the windows were covered with heavy, dark plastic, giving the appearance from the outside that the building was deserted.

They walked down a short hallway and entered a small room. There were five people in the room. Two she recognized: the gruff, battle-scarred Colonel Sawyer and Mack O'Shea. There were two other men and a woman.

For a moment, Mack's gaze met hers and held. She felt a surge of emotion and a shiver race down her spine. There were stormy emotions in Mack's eyes that she couldn't interpret. He suddenly looked away from her.

Nicholson introduced Dusty to the group. He gave the name of the other two men as Berkley and Martin, the names on their passports, no doubt fictitious. They had the look of men accustomed to action and violence. She thought they were probably Vietnam veterans or ex-undercover policemen. The woman was Margaret Jackson, the helicopter pilot, a slim, suntanned woman in her mid-thirties. Dusty knew they had all entered the country under assumed identities and with doctored passports, a very risky business that, in itself, could land them in prison.

Mack slowly uncoiled his big frame from a chair and stood before the group. A hard lump filled Dusty's throat as she gazed at his broad shoulders, his unruly dark red hair and his rugged features.

He pointed to a map on the wall, jabbing his forefinger at a circle. "According to the informant, the kidnappers are holed up in an old abandoned banana plantation about ten miles from here."

One of the men, Berkley, sneered. "Are we really going to swallow that story? The informant was probably one of Julio's cousins, making a fast buck off gullible Americans."

Colonel Sawyer rose, his heavy brows drawn in a fierce scowl. His voice was so strident it rattled the tin sides of the building. "I thought the same thing until he showed me this." He tossed the Polaroid snapshot of Emory Wilson to Berkley.

"There's further corroboration," Mack added. "Today I spotted a CIA agent in a bar downtown, a good friend I knew when I was with the department. I showed him the map Julio's friend gave us. He backed it up. He said the information he'd been able to get pointed to the same location."

"Then what are we waiting for?" Berkley demanded. "Let's hit the place."

"What do you propose we do, go chuck rocks at them?" Colonel Sawyer barked, the corner of his lips drawn down in a sour expression. "With the tight security at the airport and border checkpoints, we weren't able to smuggle so much as a peashooter into the country."

"Well, then, what the hell are we doing here?" Berkley asked.

"Pipe down," Sawyer snapped. "I was about to add that this morning I gave Julio a wad of money. He's out shopping the black market for arms."

"I still don't trust the guy," Berkley said. "Okay, maybe the map is authentic. Maybe that deserted plantation is where they're holding Emory. But we don't know if Julio is going to show up with the guns."

"I think he is," Bob Nicholson suddenly said, his voice soft when compared to the ground-shaking bass rumble of Colonel Sawyer. "Julio is after more than just stealing the money we gave him for the guns. He's after a reward I promised. More than that, he's got his sights set on getting to America, and he's got it in his head that we might be his ticket there. The way I have Julio sized up is that he's an opportunist. He may not have much formal education, but he's streetwise and he has a mind that's keen, sharp and ambitious. He's had us spotted from the very first minute. Think about it. All the other Americans are getting out of this country as fast as they possibly can. Even the embassy personnel are leaving. Yet here a group of a half dozen of us are coming into the country. Obviously we're not tourists. Julio put two and two together and smelled some kind of American operation involving big money. That's why he's been following us around town, why he showed up to rescue Mrs. O'Shea and me from that mob. He probably followed us to the embassy and the police station. He wasn't far behind the whole time.''

"All right," Colonel Sawyer thundered, "let's go on the assumption that this Julio kid is going to show up with the hardware. Here's the plan. We have three company Jeeps, plus the helicopter if we can bribe enough army personnel to look the other way when Margaret takes it up. We'll need the four-wheel-drive Jeeps because the roads out to that old banana plantation are little more than dirt paths through the jungle and after all this rain they'll be gumbo. We leave the city about midnight tomorrow night. Mr. Nicholson is giving everyone a bundle of money to bribe any military personnel who try to stop you because you're out after curfew. Mack, you take this road." He pointed to the map. "Berkley and Martin will be in the second Jeep. You take this road. I'll be in the third Jeep and I'll come in from this direction. Stop within a mile of the place and wait. At exactly 0500, get out and hike. According to this map, you'll come to a clearing. The plantation house is a few hundred yards from the edge. Wait until you get my signal. I'll shoot a flare. We'll hit the house with tear gas. If the rain lets up, Margaret will be coming in with the helicopter. Everything depends on surprise—''

He was interrupted by the sound of a noisy, rattling, banging engine outside. ''Unless I'm very much mistaken,'' Dusty said, ''that's Julio's taxi.''

Sawyer went to a window, pushed the plastic aside a fraction and peered out. He nodded with a grunt and went to unlock the door.

In a few minutes, Julio entered the room, carrying a large box. He was grinning broadly. ''Julio bring everything. You help, please?''

The others went out to the taxi and carried in several armloads of equipment.

Dusty stared in amazement at the mounting pile of guns on the table. There were automatic weapons, shotguns, a box of hand grenades, even a box of dynamite.

''Where did you get all this stuff?'' Bob Nicholson gasped.

''A general steal it out of the government armory. He sells it through a black-market dealer,'' Julio explained. He grinned proudly. ''Julio do a good job, yes?''

''You did fine, kid,'' Colonel Sawyer rumbled.

''You pay big reward, now?''

"You'll definitely get the reward as soon as we make sure Emory really is being held at that deserted plantation," Nicholson exclaimed.

"Julio go along. Make sure."

"What you mean is make sure we don't skip out without paying you the reward," Sawyer grunted. "Guess I can't blame you for looking out after your own interests. Okay, you can ride in the Jeep with me."

"How you get out of country?" Julio asked. "No more airline service. Borders all closed now."

"Yes. Rescuing Emory from the kidnappers is only half the battle," Nicholson said. "We still have to get out of the country. I have my private jet at the airport, fueled and ready to take off. It's fully equipped for any contingency. We even have a doctor and nurse on board with complete medical facilities in case somebody gets hurt during this operation."

Julio looked doubtful. "Maybe army not let you take off."

"We'll have to deal with that when the time comes," Sawyer barked. "I'm counting on the general panic and anarchy that's sweeping the city. The fighting has spread from the southern part of town. By tomorrow night there'll be street fighting everywhere. *El presidente* is going to get out soon to save his hide. He sees the handwriting on the wall. The revolution is taking over. By tomorrow night there may be such chaos at the airport that nobody will try to stop us. Paying off officials will help, too.

"Remember," he added, "surprise is the key to making this a successful operation. If we catch the kidnappers sleeping just before dawn, we can pull it off. Then we make our way back here, transfer from the Jeeps to passenger cars and drive to the airport where Bob will have the jet waiting to take off."

Chapter Fourteen

The meeting ended. Lights were turned off and the group left the building. In the darkness, Mack moved to Dusty's side. "Want to ride back to the hotel with me? I'm taking one of the Jeeps."

With a wrenching pain, Dusty thought about Laura Nicholson. She was surprised Laura hadn't come out here with Mack. But no doubt the blonde was waiting for him in their hotel room.

"No, thanks," she said coldly. "I'll go back with Mr. Nicholson."

It was too dark to see the expression in Mack's eyes, but she could tell he was staring at her. There was a moment's silence, then he shrugged. "Suit yourself," he said, before he turned and walked to one of the four-wheel-drive vehicles parked beside the building.

Dusty blinked back a sudden rush of tears. *What am I doing?* she asked herself frantically. Here she was wallowing in petty jealousy when Mack could get killed within the next twenty-four hours. This wasn't a movie set in which Grant Packer was playing the part of a tough guy. This was for real. They wouldn't be shooting blanks like on a movie set; there'd be real bullets that could tear through flesh and bone. There wouldn't be any stuntmen; Mack and the others would be playing the dangerous parts—parts that could end in death.

Suddenly coming face to face with possible death could put a lot of things into perspective. As hurt and angry as she was over Laura Nicholson, those emotions took a temporary back seat to fear.

I have to be there. Whatever has come between Mack and me, he's still the man I love. No one can ever take his place. I need to be at his side, whatever happens, to help him if I can....

Laura might make Mack a good wife as far as helping him in his job and running his home, Dusty thought. But Laura wouldn't be worth a plug nickle tomorrow night. Violence and danger were no strangers to Dusty. She thought about the times she and Mack had faced danger together—in the mideast, in the jet hijacking, in the wilds of the Sierra Madres and the bandits' lair. Those were the times they had been the closest—a closeness that Laura would never know. Times like this, Mack needed somebody like Dusty at his side; not a wife who read *Better Homes and Gardens*.

She wiped the tears from her eyes and walked to Bob Nicholson's car.

As they were driving back to the hotel, Nicholson said, "I hope I'm not intruding in your personal life, Mrs. O'Shea, but Mack is almost like a son to me. Since I've come to know you, I have a great deal of respect and admiration for you. You're a fine young woman with strong character and integrity. I know about the difficulty you and Mack are having. I'm sorry."

"I suppose Laura has talked with you about us," Dusty muttered.

"Well, of course I'm aware of how Laura feels. She and Mack have known each other for years. At one time they were engaged. But I try not to interfere in my daughter's private life. She's a grown woman now. I tried to dissuade her from coming down here. It was foolhardy for her to expose herself to this kind of danger, but she had her mind made up.

"Anyway, at the present time, all I can think about is saving Emory's life. I realize that as far as you're concerned, Emory Wilson is just a name in the newspaper headlines. When you write your story, I'd like for you to know this man as a fine, decent human being. There hasn't been a more loyal employee in the company. His wife, Ellen, is a lovely, talented woman. They have two children, a boy and a girl. The boy is ten, the girl eight. They miss their father. They're so worried..."

Nicholson paused, his voice filled with emotion. He struck the steering wheel angrily with his fist. "I can't let Emory down. I can't let any of my people down. And we can't let Americans down. This situation is more than just a single kidnapping. We can't let kidnappers and political terrorists think American businessmen are easy targets! We have to fight back! We have to send them a message that when they attack Americans, somebody is going to take action.''

Dusty was so worried that she had hardly heard him. She agreed wholeheartedly with what he was saying, but her thoughts were on Mack. ''I want to go along tomorrow night when Mack and the others raid the kidnappers' hideout.''

Nicholson looked surprised. He frowned and shook his head. ''I'm sorry. We can't let you do that.''

''But why not? If I'm going to do a good job on this story, I need to see everything firsthand—especially the rescue attempt.''

''It's too dangerous,'' Nicholson said flatly.

''I've been in dangerous situations before. It goes with the job.''

''I'm sorry, Mrs. O'Shea, but I can't permit it. I'm worried enough about the people involved in this rescue operation, but at least they're professionals trained in police and military operations. They've volunteered, knowing the risks.''

''I know the risks. I'm volunteering.''

Nicholson shook his head. ''It's out of the question. Besides the risk to you, it would complicate the operation. Every move has been carefully planned. Each man has a specific function. They can't be distracted by an extra woman.''

''I'm not just a woman,'' Dusty fumed. ''I'm a journalist. Besides, your helicopter pilot is a woman.''

''That's different. She's been through the same training as the others. You'll just have to be content with getting information secondhand. Tomorrow night you can go to the airport with me. You'll be there when the team arrives with Emory, early in the morning hours, if all goes well. You'll be a witness at the briefing, hear everything that happened. You'll be the first reporter in the world to get the story. That should make you very happy.''

I'd be a lot happier at Mack's side, Dusty thought, but she dropped the argument. She could see Nicholson was not likely to change his mind.

When they pulled into the hotel's multitiered parking garage, Dusty saw that Mack had beat them back. The Jeep he was driving was parked in the line of cars near where Nicholson stopped his car.

The next day Dusty moved restlessly around the hotel, looking out at the torrential rain that had not let up. She was overwhelmed with worry and frustration.

She considered pleading with Nicholson again, but decided it was useless. And Mack certainly wouldn't take her with him, considering the danger involved.

She went for a walk in the rain again, trying to work off some of her inner turmoil. Coming back from the walk, she entered the hotel through the parking garage. She saw Mack's Jeep where he'd parked it the night before. Thoughtfully, she walked over and had a closer look. Some objects in the back seat were covered with a heavy tarp, probably rope, flashlights, guns and ammunition.

Dusty returned to her room, still chafing. As she lay on her bed, staring at the ceiling and listening to the rain drumming against her windowpane, she had what she considered to be a brilliant idea. A smile played around her lips.

She lay there until night fell. Then, wearing jeans, shirt and boots and carrying her raincoat and camera bag, she left her room. She stopped at the snack-dispensing machine, dropped in some coins and stuffed candy bars in her pocket.

Then she walked downstairs, through the lobby and into the dimly lit parking garage. No one was around. She went over to Mack's Jeep, got in the back seat and hid by pulling the tarp over her as she settled down to wait.

Chapter Fifteen

The hours dragged by. Dusty grew stiff and sore in the small, cramped space. The tarp smelled bad. A hard object jabbed her in the back. She might come out of this permanently crippled, she thought miserably.

In spite of her discomfort, she dozed off for a while. She was awakened suddenly when the door opened. She heard the starter grind and the engine rumble into life. Then she was jerked forward. A hard object jabbed her back before she was thrown back. She held on for dear life, but she was elated. Mack had gotten in the Jeep and had driven out of the garage without noticing her.

For a while the ride wasn't too bad, but then they reached the end of the paved roads and started down a soggy dirt lane filled with holes. Dusty was slammed around like a sack of grain. She was going to be black and blue from head to foot if she lived through this, she thought grimly.

She considered letting Mack know she was in the back seat, but decided against it. He might just be stubborn enough to turn around and take her back to the hotel. She gritted her teeth and clung to the seat. Somehow she had to hang on until they'd gone so far that Mack wouldn't have time to take her back.

The agonizing ride seemed to last forever. Then, suddenly, they came to a jolting halt.

The engine died and there was the shock of sudden, utter silence. After a few moments, she heard the creepy night sounds of the jungle, the call of birds and the rustle of animals in the thick growth.

The Jeep sagged. A door opened.

Suddenly, the tarp was pulled back. Dusty saw the dim outlines of Mack's head. He was standing there, frozen. She could just make out the expression of un-believing shock on his face.

A flashlight beam blinded her. "Hi," she said, warding off the light with her hand.

"Dusty, I'm going to break your damn neck," Mack said in the most exasperated growl she'd ever heard.

"You almost did already. You're the worst driver I've ever known. I don't think you missed a single pothole all the way out here. Do you mind getting that blamed light out of my eyes?"

She untangled herself from the rope and boxes and crawled painfully from the back seat. "Oh, my ach-ing back," she groaned, slowly straightening to a standing position. She limped in a circle, trying to get some feeling back in her left foot, which had gone to sleep.

Mack's big hands stopped her, crushing her shoulders in an angry grip. He looked furious. "You had orders to stay at the hotel."

"So I disobeyed orders. Court-martial me."

He shook his head, at a loss for words. Finally he said, "You'll go to any lengths for a story, won't you?"

Tears suddenly blinded her. "Do you think that's the only reason I came with you?"

"What other possible reason could you have?"

"Never mind," she said angrily. "Listen, can we get in out of the rain? I'm getting soaked."

They got back in the Jeep. The rain continued to drum on the cloth top.

For a while they sat in angry silence. Then Dusty said, "For your information, I did not hide in the Jeep just to get a news story. I—I was worried about you. I wanted to be around in case you needed help."

He stared at her. "I don't believe you."

"Well, it's the truth. I'm afraid you'll get your stupid head blown off." Again she blinked back tears.

Mack frowned. He looked at her, then away. "Why should you care if I die? I'm not Grant Packer."

Dusty pressed her lips together angrily. She looked at him in the darkness. "That's another thing I want to clear up," she said. "I didn't want you getting into this dangerous operation filled with a lot of wrong ideas about me and Grant Packer."

"What do you mean, 'wrong ideas'?"

"There is absolutely nothing going on between me and Grant Packer. Surely you don't believe gossip!"

Mack looked back at her with a troubled expression. "What am I supposed to believe?"

"The truth, Mack. I simply went out there to interview the guy. He did get kind of interested in me and we were together some, but I never for a minute had any romantic feelings for him. We certainly weren't having an affair. I want to make you understand that before the shooting starts."

There was a lengthy silence.

"Well, do you believe me?"

Mack nodded slowly. It was dark, but she thought she saw relief in his eyes. "Yes, Dusty," he said, his voice strangely soft. "Yes, I do believe you. I'm—I'm glad."

"Not that it should make all that much difference," she said bitterly. "All you have on your mind these days is Laura Nicholson, anyway."

Mack frowned. "While we're clearing things up, let's get that matter straightened out, too. Nothing is going on between Laura and me."

"Oh, come on! She flew down here with you. She's sharing your hotel room, isn't she?"

"Do you believe that?"

"Well, isn't she?"

"Did you check the register?"

"I didn't have to. She came to my room for a girl-to-girl talk. She said you and she had a quote understanding unquote. She as good as said that all you were waiting for was our divorce and then the two of you were getting married."

Mack sighed. "You don't want me to believe the tabloids, yet you believe everything she tells you."

"Well, why shouldn't I?"

"Because it's not true. I realized when I fell in love with you that I never loved Laura. I'm not in love with her now; I never was. Even if you and I get a divorce, I wouldn't marry her. It wouldn't be fair to either one of us, especially not her. I've been her friend, yes, but that's all. If she's reading more into it than that it's just because she doesn't want to take no for an answer."

"Is—is that the truth, Mack O'Shea?"

"Listen, Dusty, you're right about tonight. I wish you hadn't come but now that you're here, we have to face the fact that it's going to be dangerous. There's the possibility that one or both of us could get hurt—maybe killed. Times like this, people tell the truth. I'm telling you the truth now. I don't love Laura. I've been awfully mad at you at times, but I've never stopped loving you."

Dusty tried to swallow, but the lump in her throat was too large. Tears ran down her cheeks. "I—I guess like you said once, we're hooked on each other, huh?"

"I guess."

Mack opened his shirt. Around his neck was a string. On the end of the string was the wedding ring she had pinned to the pillow next to him that night in Monterrey. Now he broke the string. He held her hand and tenderly slipped the ring back on her finger. "Whatever happens to our marriage, I want you to wear this tonight, Dusty."

She was too filled with emotion to speak. She pressed the ring against her cheek, tears spilling over. She looked up into his eyes. "It—it feels good. I missed it. It seems to belong there, doesn't it?"

"Yes . . . it does."

"Do you think you could kiss me now?"

His arms went around her, drawing her closer. Their lips met tenderly, lovingly.

"Oh, Mack," she whispered against his lips. "Why is it we're always so close at times like this when we're liable to die at any minute?"

"Maybe we feel things more intensely."

"Yeah, we get along fine when there's a crisis. It's when everything's okay that we get into trouble."

"Let's not talk about it now." He kissed her again.

Her arms went around his neck and she held him fiercely as if somehow her slim body could protect him from the dangers they would be facing in a few hours.

"Hey," Mack exclaimed, "the rain is letting up. That means Margaret can bring in the helicopter." He consulted his watch. "Let's get going."

From the back seat, he took two automatic weapons. "Do you know how to use a hand grenade?"

"Sure. Don't pull the pin until you're ready to chuck it."

"Stick this pistol in your belt."

Dusty took the pistol he handed her, thrust it in her belt and slung her camera bag over a shoulder.

"The pistol is just for protection," Mack warned her. "I don't want you getting involved in the shooting. You stay back where it's safe."

They left the Jeep and began following a dim path through the jungle growth. Dusty felt the wet branches and vines slapping her. She thought about the poisonous reptiles, the panthers and other wild beasts and shrank closer to Mack.

His flashlight picked out a faint trail.

At last the growth became less dense. Then they reached the edge of the clearing.

"Shh," Mack cautioned. He pointed to the dark shape of a building. "That's it," he whispered. "The abandoned house. If our information is right, that's where the kidnappers are holding Emory Wilson."

Then Mack said, "Smear this on your face."

"What is it?"

"Burnt cork. Helps hide your face."

"It'll mess up my makeup."

"Your makeup will get messed up more if they draw a bead on the pale outline of your face."

The sky was starting to lighten with the first hint of dawn.

"I wonder if the others are here," Dusty said nervously. "I'd hate to think of just the two of us storming the place."

"We'll soon find out."

Slow minutes dragged by.

Suddenly, from the other side of the clearing, a flare streaked into the sky.

"That's it!" Mack cried. "Now we have to get to Emory before the kidnappers harm him. You stay here."

Mack leapt to his feet and broke into a run toward the building.

Dusty grabbed a camera from her bag. She fitted an electronic flash into place. Then, ignoring Mack's command, she ran close on his heels.

She saw the others racing toward the building from different directions: Colonel Sawyer, Berkley, Martin. They were running low to the ground, carrying their rifles. Then Dusty heard the sound of an approaching helicopter. Right on schedule, Margaret Jackson was bringing in the chopper.

Colonel Sawyer reached the building first. With a hoarse bellow, he smashed the front door in with a heavy boot.

Dusty began snapping pictures. The flashes winked in the darkness.

Inside the building, there were harsh, startled shouts. They raced down a hallway, jerking open doors. Flashlight beams slashed the darkness. Dusty heard the blast of gunfire. She saw a slim figure in a T-shirt stamped with the name of an American rock band run to the building. "Julio!" she gasped.

Mack leapt across the porch, smashed a window with his gun butt and crawled in. Dusty went in right after him. Men were cursing, hurling furniture. Dusty remembered the odds. They were outnumbered two to one. But they had surprise on their side.

Mack kicked a door in. Dusty followed him into a room. There, on a couch, was an American, unshaven and pale. He sat up, looking frightened and confused.

"Emory Wilson?" Mack asked.

The American nodded.

Dusty's camera recorded the dramatic moment.

Colonel Sawyer stormed into the room at that point. "Come on, man, get up. We're here to get you out of this mess."

An expression of wonder and hope filled Wilson's eyes. "I—I can't get up," he said, nodding to his bound feet.

Sawyer muttered a curse. He whipped out a wicked-looking knife, cut the ropes from Wilson's feet and arms and helped him to stand. With Wilson's arm over his shoulder, Sawyer started out of the room, a Colt .45 held menacingly in his big fist.

The terrorists, now awake and armed, were pouring into the room. Everything was darkness and confusion. Suddenly a man's swarthy, bearded face, distorted with rage, loomed before Dusty. He was holding a pistol aimed straight at her. Without thinking, she pointed her camera and pressed the shutter release. The electronic flash made a blinding splash of light. The kidnapper staggered backward, temporarily blinded by the intense flash. Dusty picked up a board and brought it down on his hand, knocking the pistol to the floor.

A heavy body slammed against her, throwing her to the ground. Half-stunned, she looked up to see Mack struggling with one of the men. Then, to her horror, she saw one of the terrorists holding a knife as he moved toward Mack. He raised the knife, bringing it down toward Mack's unprotected back.

Dusty scrambled on the floor for the pistol she had knocked from the terrorist's hand. She swung it up and fired. The man with the knife dropped it with a howl, clutching his arm.

Mack dispatched his opponent with a hard right and knelt beside Dusty. "Damn, you're a dead shot. Remind me never to get in an argument with you when you're holding a gun."

"You can thank my brothers when you see them. They taught me how to shoot. Has the colonel gotten Wilson out of the building?"

"Yes. Thank God he's safe. Colonel Sawyer is taking him out to the helicopter. Let's get out of here."

Dusty scrambled to her feet. Suddenly she screamed, "Mack, look out!"

One of the kidnappers had burst through the door. He was holding a pistol aimed at Mack. He squeezed the trigger.

Dusty threw herself in front of Mack. She felt a heavy blow and went numb. Dimly she heard Mack call her name right before he pulled the trigger on his automatic weapon. The terrorist fell back through the doorway.

Then Mack scooped her up in his arms and ran from the building.

"My camera!" Dusty gasped.

"I've got it," Mack reassured her.

To Dusty, everything was happening in a kind of unreal slow motion. She didn't feel any pain. She felt numb and dazed. She heard the colonel's voice thunder, "Everyone out? Good."

Some of the terrorists were starting out of the building. "I fix!" Julio shouted. He yanked the pin of a grenade and hurled it at the building. There was a deafening blast that shattered windows. The old building seemed to shudder. The porch came crashing down.

"Berkley, Martin, Julio," the colonel shouted, "come with me. We're going back in the Jeeps. Margaret, you take Emory and the girl. She's been shot. Mack, you'd better stay with her."

Dusty couldn't remember the helicopter ride to the airport. She was vaguely conscious of Mack carrying her to Nicholson's waiting jet. Then she was in a small, cramped emergency room. A doctor and nurse were working over her. Mack was holding her hand. She saw the worry in his eyes and tried to squeeze his hand reassuringly but there wasn't any strength in her hand.

Somehow she managed a smile. "You look pretty silly with that burned cork on your face."

Mack was crying. "Dusty, I love you."

"I love you, too," she whispered. "See...I told you you needed to have me with you."

"I guess you were right. You saved my life."

"Lie still," the doctor ordered. "Don't talk."

"Do you think you could give me some kind of shot?" she asked weakly. "All of a sudden I'm starting to hurt real bad."

A needle pricked her arm. She felt dizzy, but the pain eased. "When are we taking off?" she whispered.

"As soon as the others get here. They're coming by car. It takes longer."

"Is Emory Wilson safe?"

"Yes. The doctor has checked him over and given him a sedative."

The injection was making Dusty drowsy.

Then a commotion outside roused her.

"What's happening?" she whispered.

"Colonel Sawyer and the others just arrived. They were getting in the plane when a carload of soldiers drove up. A major got out and told Colonel Sawyer we were not permitted to take off."

"What did Colonel Sawyer do?"

"He told the major he outranked him. Then he punched him out."

Dusty could feel the movement of the jet.

"We're taking off," Mack told her. "Just lie still, Dusty. We'll have you in an American hospital in a few hours."

"Did everyone get on the plane?"

"Yes. Even Julio."

"What's that popping sound?"

"The soldiers are shooting at us, but don't be frightened. We're at the far end of the runway by now and they're notoriously bad shots."

Moments later, there was the smooth feeling of being airborne.

Dusty was sitting in a hospital bed, her shoulder swathed in bandages. She was gazing through a window, watching snowflakes drift down, thinking how strange it was that only a few days ago she had been in ninety-degree weather in South America.

"You have a visitor," a nurse said, poking her head in.

Mack entered the room with a bag under one arm.

Dusty smiled at him, feeling suddenly warm and glad inside. "Hi. I was getting lonely."

Mack nodded. He patted her head clumsily. His eyes, moist, gazed at her, saying much more than his groping words. "You're looking swell, Dusty."

"No, I'm not. I look like hell. But I'm getting better. What's in the bag?"

Mack emptied the contents on the bed. Candy bars, cookies, bags of potato chips, pretzels and doughnuts spilled out.

"All my favorite junk foods," Dusty cried, her eyes misty. "How sweet. Gee, thank you, Mack!"

"I figured you deserved a treat after saving my life."

"Thank you for all the flowers, too. My room has been looking like a florist's shop."

Mack stood beside the bed, looking down at her as if he had to keep filling his eyes with the sight of her.

"Everybody get home safe?"

"Yes. Emory Wilson is back with his family. Colonel Sawyer and the others are fine."

"Julio?"

"Oh, Julio is making out like a bandit. Bob gave him that reward. Five hundred thousand dollars. Julio's dream came true. He's a rich American. Well . . . not an American yet, but Bob's trying to pull some strings with the state department. Meanwhile, Julio is running around, seeing Disneyworld and all the sights. He can't decide if he wants to start his own rock band or a taxi company."

Dusty laughed. "More power to him. We couldn't have pulled it off without him."

"Or you," Mack said. "I bet those terrorists will think twice before they tangle with a Cherokee on the warpath."

"Mack!"

"Oh, about your pictures. Myra said to tell you she's getting a fabulous price for them. They're incredible shots of the rescue. You're sure to get an impressive award, maybe a Pulitzer prize."

"That's good news."

He was holding her hand, the one with her wedding ring. He held it gently, tenderly in his big, strong fingers. Dusty saw tears in his eyes.

"Dusty, what are we going to do about us?"

"I—I don't know, Mack. What *are* we going to do about us?"

"Beats me. We're hooked on each other, aren't we?"

"Seems that way."

"But I know you. After your shoulder heals, you're going off on some crazy assignment again."

"Maybe."

"We'll fight about it and we'll separate and then we'll get back together...."

There was a silence.

Mack squeezed her hand. "I love you, Dusty. I couldn't ever love anybody else."

"I feel the same way, Mack."

"I guess we'll have to settle for that for now and take each day as it comes."

"Okay. As long as you keep loving me, it'll work out somehow."

There was another silence.

Dusty smiled. "Want a doughnut?"

Silhouette Special Edition
COMING NEXT MONTH

CRISTEN'S CHOICE—Ginna Gray
Finding a blatantly virile, nearly naked man in her bathroom gave Cristen the shock of her life. But Ryan O'Malley's surprises didn't stop there, and his teasing sensual tactics left her limp with longing—and perpetually perplexed!

PURPLE DIAMONDS—Jo Ann Algermissen
When beautiful heartbreaker Halley Twain was assigned to his ward, Dr. Mark Abraham knew she meant danger. After reopening his old emotional wounds, would she have the healing touch to save him?

WITH THIS RING—Pat Warren
Nick flipped over kooky Kate Stevens, but she was his brother's girlfriend, and the two men already had a score to settle. Still, Nick couldn't stop himself from wanting her.

RENEGADE SON—Lisa Jackson
With her farm in jeopardy, Dani would do anything to save it. But when sexy, rugged Chase McEnroe seemed determined to take it from her, she wondered just how far she'd have to go....

A MEASURE OF LOVE—Lindsay McKenna
Jessie had come to protect wild horses, but one look at proud, defiant rancher Rafe Kincaid was enough to warn her—it was her heart that was in danger.

HIGH SOCIETY—Lynda Trent
Their families had feuded for years, but mechanic Mike Barlow and socialite Sheila Danforth felt nothing but attraction. Could the heat of their kisses ever melt society's icy disdain?

AVAILABLE NOW:

FIRE AT DAWN
Linda Shaw

THE SHOWGIRL AND THE PROFESSOR
Phyllis Halldorson

HONORABLE INTENTIONS
Kate Meriwether

DANGER IN HIS ARMS
Patti Beckman

THEIR SONG UNENDING
Anna James

RETURN TO EDEN
Jeanne Stephens

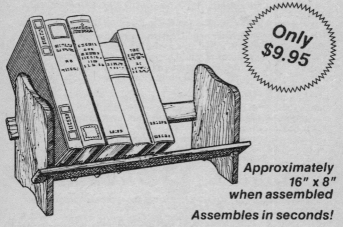

Take 4 Silhouette Romance novels

FREE

Then preview 6 brand-new Silhouette Romance® novels—delivered to your door as soon as they are published—for 15 days without obligation. When you decide to keep them, pay just $1.95 each, *with no shipping, handling or other charges of any kind!*

Each month, you'll meet lively young heroines and share in their thrilling escapades, trials and triumphs...virile men you'll find as attractive and irresistible as the heroines do...and colorful supporting characters you'll feel you've always known.

Start with 4 Silhouette Romance novels absolutely FREE. They're yours to keep without obligation, and you can cancel at any time.

As an added bonus, you'll also get the Silhouette Books Newsletter FREE with every shipment. Every issue is filled with news on upcoming books, interviews with your favorite authors, even their favorite recipes.

Simply fill out and return the coupon today!
This offer is not available in Canada.

Silhouette Books, 120 Brighton Rd., P.O. Box 5084, Clifton, NJ 07015-5084

Clip and mail to: Silhouette Books,
120 Brighton Road, P.O. Box 5084, Clifton, NJ 07015-5084

YES. Please send me 4 Silhouette Romance novels FREE. Unless you hear from me after I receive them, send me six new Silhouette Romance novels to preview each month as soon as they are published. I understand you will bill me just $1.95 each (a total of $11.70) with no shipping, handling, or other charges of any kind. There is no minimum number of books that I must buy, and I can cancel at any time. The first 4 books are mine to keep.   B1RS87

Name	(please print)	
Address		Apt. #
City	State	Zip

Terms and prices subject to change. Not available in Canada.   SilR-SUB-1A
SILHOUETTE ROMANCE is a service mark and registered trademark.

Take 4 Silhouette Intimate Moments novels FREE

Then preview 4 brand new Silhouette Intimate Moments® novels —delivered to your door every month—for 15 days as soon as they are published. When you decide to keep them, you pay just $2.25 each ($2.50 each, in Canada), *with no shipping, handling, or other charges of any kind!*

Silhouette Intimate Moments novels are not for everyone. They were created to give you a more detailed, more exciting reading experience, filled with romantic fantasy, intense sensuality, and stirring passion.

The first 4 Silhouette Intimate Moments novels are absolutely FREE and without obligation, yours to keep. You can cancel at any time.

You'll also receive a FREE subscription to the Silhouette Books Newsletter as long as you remain a member. Each issue is filled with news on upcoming titles, interviews with your favorite authors, even their favorite recipes.

To get your 4 FREE books, fill out and mail the coupon today!

Silhouette Intimate Moments®

Silhouette Books, 120 Brighton Rd., P.O. Box 5084, Clifton, NJ 07015-5084

**Clip and mail to: Silhouette Books,
120 Brighton Road, P.O. Box 5084, Clifton, NJ 07015-5084**•

YES. Please send me 4 FREE Silhouette Intimate Moments novels. Unless you hear from me after I receive them, send me 4 brand new Silhouette Intimate Moments novels to preview each month. I understand you will bill me just $2.25 each, a total of $9.00 (in Canada, $2.50 each, a total of $10.00)—with no shipping, handling, or other charges of any kind. There is no minimum number of books that I must buy, and I can cancel at any time. The first 4 books are mine to keep. *Silhouette Intimate Moments available in Canada through subscription only.*

BIM587

Name _____ (please print)

Address _____ Apt. #_____

City _____ State/Prov. _____ Zip/Postal Code_____

* In Canada, mail to: Silhouette Canadian Book Club,
320 Steelcase Rd., E., Markham, Ontario, L3R 2M1, Canada   IM-SUB-1A
Terms and prices subject to change.
SILHOUETTE INTIMATE MOMENTS is a service mark and registered trademark.

FOUR UNIQUE SERIES FOR EVERY WOMAN YOU ARE...

Silhouette Romance

Heartwarming romances that will make you laugh and cry as they bring you all the wonder and magic of falling in love.

6 titles per month

Silhouette Special Edition

Expanded romances written with emotion and heightened romantic tension to ensure powerful stories. A rare blend of passion and dramatic realism.

6 titles per month

Silhouette Desire

Believable, sensuous, compelling—and above all, romantic—these stories deliver the promise of love, the guarantee of satisfaction.

6 titles per month

Silhouette Intimate Moments

Love stories that entice; longer, more sensuous romances filled with adventure, suspense, glamour and melodrama.

4 titles per month

Silhouette Romances
not available in retail outlets in Canada

SIL-GEN-1A